CHERRINGHAM

A COSY MYSTERY SERIES

SNOWBLIND

Neil Richards • Matthew Costello

RED DOG
UK

ISBN 978-1-913331-68-9

www.reddogpress.co.uk

Cherringham is a long-running mystery series set in the Cotswolds. The stories are self-contained, though many will enjoy reading them in order of publication:

1.

A LOVELY NIGHT FOR A WALK

ARCHY FLEMING PUSHED at the branches in his way.

What happened to the path I was on? he wondered.

The night had been so nice! It had been nice, hadn't it? Maybe a bit chilly. But now, so much colder, and it didn't seem like such a nice night *at all.*

He looked down. Was that a path? He couldn't tell, not with all the broken branches and leaves underfoot. Paths were usually clearer than this, weren't they? All the people walking on them, going from... going from—

Where did I come from? he wondered. *Back there, somewhere?*

There were other people there, but though he could see their faces, their smiles, he couldn't remember any of their names.

Maybe he should turn around? Go back there. But then if this was a path... maybe it led somewhere. *Had* to lead somewhere.

A village! A place to get warm, a pub! Yes! Has to be a pub ahead. With a roaring fireplace.

He thought of those words: *roaring fireplace.*

He kept stepping forwards. A thin branch that he hadn't seen snapped back and slapped him in the face, and it stung.

That's when he noticed that the trees, the path, the leaves on the ground had all turned white!

It's snowing.

He did something he remembered from long ago.

Archy stuck out his tongue, letting the flakes land on it. First a few, then more, until he could see that this was no gentle snow.

Not just a couple of soft flakes landing on his dry, cracked tongue.

No, this snow was heavy, coming down hard. And though his slippers protected his feet, right at his exposed ankles, the snow landed and stuck.

Already the snow had made the ground disappear.

His thin robe did little now. That robe — a deep mix of dark red-and-blue stripes — also had snow sticking to it.

Roaring fireplace.

And a pint.

Like a pint, I would.

He'd stand by that fireplace, and sip his pint.

In his robe. His slippers. Let all that snow melt away.

As if it hadn't been snowing at all.

Archy kept walking, his whole body shaking with each step, driven by the idea that ahead, at the end of this now-white trail, there was a village, and a pub, and all he had to do — no matter how cold he felt — was keep on going the way he was going.

HE FELL, HARD, right onto his knees, his now untrustworthy knees, kneeling in the snow, his grey hair covered in the white stuff.

Archy looked around.

Where was the damn path?

It looked like it could go to the right. That looked *sort* of like a path.

(He remained kneeling. Didn't want to get up until he knew where he was going.)

Or to the left! Right! *There's* a path, narrow, but yes he could see it, the trees with their snow-covered limbs so close, trying to hide it.

No. Straight ahead was the way. Of course. *That* was the path. Just needed to keep going in the direction he was going.

He looked around for something to grab to help pull himself to a standing position.

A craggy bush nearby. Dried berries still on its branches. He grabbed at a twisted handful of the bush's branches and pulled, using it to get off one knee.

He had the thought: *what if I can't get up?*

What if I end up staying here?

And that thought made Archy's gnarled hands grab as tight as he could, hold the branches fast, as he struggled to a standing position again.

Then, as if rewarded for his great effort, he stood shivering, shaking and he saw lights ahead. Two lights! There — and then gone.

Then again.

The village! The pub!

Close now. Close.

And Archy Fleming stumbled ahead, letting branches swipe at his face since he knew he had to go fast, not caring about the painful scratches.

He was close to the village. And all he had to do was keep going straight.

2.

THE BLIZZARD

"GETTING BAD OUT there, Jack?" Ellie said from behind the bar, looking at the Ploughman's front windows, to the snowstorm outside.

Jack turned and looked at the near-empty pub. "Where is everybody?"

"Not used to big snowstorms I guess. Everyone getting all cosy at home. Fancy another?"

"No. It really is coming down. I better get back to the Goose."

Ellie looked at two old men sitting off in a corner. "Think I should tell that lot over there to get going as well. Time to close up and head to my own fireplace. They say it's going to be a real blizzard."

Jack turned back to her. "Good idea. You know, all that snow outside... reminds me of home. We get storms like this all the time."

"I've heard. So then you're used to it. Know when to get out the snow-ploughs, salt, right? Not sure how little Cherringham will fare."

"It'll be interesting."

Jack pulled on a cloth cap and buttoned up his pea coat.

He had worn his wellies so he'd have no problem walking through the slushy stuff.

But driving? That could be a different story.

"Be safe, Ellie."

"You bet," she said, as she stepped out from around the bar and started turning lights off, finally making the two — what would the locals call them? — *geezers* start moving.

Hope they don't have far to go, Jack thought.

As the line goes... *ain't a fit night out for man nor beast.*

And, as he quickly discovered, not a fit night for his Sprite.

Back in New York, he had driven a big SUV that had no trouble handling ice, snow, rain — *whatever.*

And though he had put winter tyres on his small sports car, he knew it didn't have a lot of weight to get through the snowy roads.

As he backed out of the Ploughman's car park, he could feel those tyres struggling with the snow.

Think I was a bit too cavalier about this, Jack thought.

Back in NYC, he actually liked it when a big storm came. Brought out the best in the people; everyone pulling together. And the way snow could muffle the noisy city, covering it with a white blanket... that was something to see.

But even though he didn't have far to go to get to his boat, he could tell he'd have to take it nice and slow.

One thing: there didn't seem to be anyone else on the road. No ploughs yet.

Everyone hunkering down at home.

A Cherringham blizzard.

He looked forward to getting back to the Grey Goose and enjoying the storm from there.

JACK TOOK THE old familiar road that led that led down toward the river and the Goose.

Although, in this storm it didn't look familiar at all.

On either side, the hedges looked like a line of snowmen; the heavy, wet snow sticking fast.

He had tested the brakes — very easy with a few gentle pumps. No anti-locking brakes on this vintage item. The only way he could make them *not* lock was by taking it slow.

He remembered an old rule delivered to him by his dad when he faced his first Brooklyn winter as driver.

His father's brogue always more pronounced when he became excited about a subject.

"Now, Jack — if you ever begin to skid, you gotta remember to turn into *the skid, you understand? Into it, then slowly out of it."*

More than once he had forgotten those instructions and nearly sent his first car — a beat-up Ford Pinto — careening towards the sidewalk.

Now, he took things smoothly. Just a bit of a slip there, but he could see the tracks made by the few other cars that had passed by.

The road was deserted now though, and his windshield wipers — small, matching the car itself — struggled to keep the wet snow from building up on the windshield.

"Okay," he said to himself. "Nearly home."

He reminded himself about how a storm as beautiful and big as this one could, in a heartbeat, turn dangerous.

Considering the state of things, he might end up holed up on the Goose for a few days.

No problem there. Got his martini ingredients, a few steaks in the freezer. Plenty of food for Riley.

"Be just fine," he said again, liking the way his voice made the silence inside and out less intimidating.

He came to the curve where the fields to the right gave way to woods, a notorious spot which caught many a driver unawares even in the best weather.

Into the curve... so slowly.

When he saw someone, suddenly, a ghost-like figure, covered in the white snow — run out into the road, turning as the Sprite's headlights caught him in mid-crossing.

The figure frozen, standing there. Eyes wide.

Leaving Jack with no option other than to hit the brakes hard and turn the steering wheel.

3.

SPINOUT

AND JUST AS his father might have predicted, the Sprite began a crazy skid. Instead of turning to the right and slowing, the combination of that turn and the hitting of the brakes sent the small car spinning.

A three-sixty.

Something Jack hadn't experienced in nearly forty years.

The car had no control. Jack gently pumped the brake hoping to get it to slow even as it twirled around once, then again.

For all he knew, whoever the crazy person in the middle of the road was... he was still there, and the car would go flying at him like a pinwheel.

Jack's stomach tightened. He hated not being in control.

And this was a lot like being helpless.

But then he saw that, on the second full-circle spin, the Sprite was now sliding to the left, into the snowy hedges. Then there was a heavy bump as the tyres sank into a roadside rut.

And that rut, catching the two left tyres, at least had the effect — jarring as it was — of stopping the car.

The whole wild manoeuvre was in slow motion so Jack hadn't been thrown forward, smashing into the windshield or the steering wheel.

He looked right, trying to see the road, searching for the ghostly figure he had almost driven into.

But the side window had a coating of snow, blocking the view.

He rolled down the window, letting that coating fall into the driver's seat.

But at least he could now see the road. Deserted, as if there never had been a figure at all.

JACK OPENED THE door of the car, and got out. Snow blew sideways, nasty stuff as if trying to sneak its way into any crack in the protection offered by his coat.

Easily six or seven inches on the ground already, and still coming down thick.

"Hello!" Jack yelled.

Where was the guy who had been standing in the road?

Jack hadn't gotten a good look at him, just a glance before turning, braking.

Now — he could see the snowy circle made by the spinning car.

But there was no one there.

Jack had one thankful thought: *least I didn't hit him.*

Because if he had hit the man, the body would be lying just in front of that circle on the road.

But what was the guy doing here, running across the road?

"Hey!" he yelled.

The figure looked as if it had come from the woods ahead.

Maybe he had gone back there?

Jack started walking in that direction.

"Hey... you... you okay?"

He had competition from the wind now, whistling in his ears, and probably doing a good job of muffling his yells.

"Hello! Where are you?"

No footpath into the woods. How'd the guy come through there, pushing his way past branches, bushes?

More like he was lost.

Deeper into the woods, and Jack realised that the guy could have gone anywhere, any direction.

He stopped, did a slow turn. And outside of the whistle of the wind, and the steady falling snow, he saw and heard nothing.

Whoever it was, he thought, *let's hope he ran back where he came from.*

You wouldn't last long out here. Not in this.

He sniffed the air, then pulled his jacket collar tight to try and stop the invading snow, and walked back to the Sprite.

GETTING THE CAR out of the rut wasn't easy. He had to make it rock back and forth, all the time hearing the exposed rocky dirt grind against the undercarriage of the car.

Going to need some work after this.

But then, with one final thrust forward, the Sprite's left rear tyre got some traction and pushed the car out of the rut, back on to the road.

And as he drove the last few minutes to his boat, he kept thinking of the man who had appeared on the road, and then vanished.

He'd call Alan to alert him — and any of the crews out tonight — to keep a lookout.

But hopefully the crazy guy was already back inside his home — wherever that might be — ready to sleep it off, safe and warm.

He pulled the car in as close to the river as he could, guessing that he wouldn't be using it for a while. He could check for damage in the morning.

Then — he heard Riley barking inside.

Maybe the dog could tell that something was up outside; the storm, the wind, the snow.

Or maybe he just wanted a walk.

"Coming, boy," Jack called, hurrying from the car and up the ramp to the Grey Goose.

Riley was standing by the door, tail wagging wildly, as Jack opened it.

"Thought I was lost out there? Guess you might need a bit of walk?"

Riley knew that word and responded with an affirmative bark.

No need for a leash, and Jack led the way back down the boat ramp again as Riley bounded ahead.

Doubtful he'd want to stay out here for long.

In minutes, they were both back inside.

"YES, ALAN, the guy just stood there. Didn't get a good look at him. And when I got out, he was gone."

"Right. That is strange, Jack. Night like this, God."

"I did a bit of a search for him. Couldn't see or hear anything."

"Okay. I should be back in the village tonight; I'll take a drive around."

"Oh," said Jack. "You not here now then?"

"No, I'm in Oxford. Workshop on caring for the community."

"Good timing," said Jack.

"Tell me about it."

"Soonest you can leave, the better, I'd say Alan — it's coming down hard."

"I hear you. Anyway, the gritters should be hitting the village soon. I'll call them — get them to keep an eye out as well."

"Great. Hope he got back okay... wherever he came from."

For a second, Alan didn't say anything to that.

"Hmm. That's the thing, Jack. Not much out there. Unless he had been wandering for quite some time. Anyway, we'll keep a lookout. You okay, the car?"

"Me? I'm fine. Sprite — we'll see. Got me home at least."

"Good. Stay safe Jack."

"You too, Alan. Kinda think we might be needing you here in the next day or two."

"Do my best, Jack."

Then...

And speaking of safe...

Jack thought he'd call and check on Sarah and the kids. School had closed early and he guessed Sarah probably came home in the early afternoon as well.

But still — wouldn't hurt to see how everyone was doing.

JACK HAD PULLED up a chair by the boat's port window so he could watch all that snow come down while he talked to Sarah.

"What about Daniel — guess he's eager to get out in it?"

Sarah laughed. "He's never seen anything like this. But it's dark, still coming down. Tomorrow, I said."

"Wise decision. Going to be interesting to see how your village deals with this the day after."

"Won't be many shops open, I'd guess."

He hesitated mentioning the near run-in with the mysterious guy on the road.

But then he took a sip of his martini, a chilly drink for a chilly night.

And he told her about what happened.

"God, Jack. You okay?"

"Not a scratch. The Sprite on the other hand will need to be looked at."

"And that man—?"

"Vanished. Like he wasn't even there."

"Strange."

"Sarah, any idea where he might have come from?"

"Out there? Nearest place with people is right where you are. And you know everyone who's still in their boats this time of year, don't you?"

"Yup. And he didn't look dressed for the weather. Think... he had a bathrobe on."

"Well, you told Alan. Not much more you can do."

Another sip. He guessed that Sarah was right.

Not much more to do.

But then why did it feel as if there *was* more to be done?

"Yeah," he said. "So, you guys stay warm. Going to fix a rib eye in a bit. Kind of love nights like this."

"Have one for me!"

"You bet."

"And Jack — thanks for checking in."

"My pleasure," he said. "Speak soon."

And he knew, this call, this checking-in... was indeed a pleasure.

Closest thing he had to family here.

Riley sat at his feet, now so peaceful, head resting on his paws.

"Now for that steak, eh boy?" The dog raised his eyes but didn't stir as Jack got up and headed to the boat's small galley.

4.

THE MORNING AFTER

SARAH INSPECTED DANIEL, about to brave the world of snow outside.

"I don't think," she said with a grin, "that I've ever seen you wearing so many *layers*."

He had his puffa jacket zipped tight. Worn only once last winter, and on his head a knitted cap yanked down low. Two pairs of trousers and hiking boots, with thick socks pulled up over the bottoms of his trousers.

"I do feel a bit like the Michelin man," Daniel said grinning.

He turned to the back door, the windows glistening with morning sun.

She laughed at that. "Don't stay out there too long, it's still really cold."

Her very own Michelin boy nodded. "Going to see if I can build a fort out of the stuff. Maybe even tunnels!"

"An engineering project. Fantastic. And I'll make sure that there's hot chocolate waiting for you when you take a break."

And with that, she opened the door, and Daniel went out into what was once a small garden but now resembled an ice flow bobbing away from Antarctica.

She held the door open only a second, seeing Daniel grab his fort-building tool — a seldom-used snow shovel — and then start trudging into the feet-high snow.

Now so deep, she saw, that he could barely get his feet up and over to take a step.

They promised a blizzard, she thought, *and they delivered.*

She shut the door tight, still checking on her son loving this snow in only the way that a young boy could.

Which is when Chloe came into the kitchen.

"MUM…"

From her tone, the princess wasn't especially happy.

"Morning, Chloe."

"All this *yucky* snow. You think it will be gone in time for Lucy's party this weekend?"

Sarah glanced at the back door's window. "Don't know, love. There's a lot of snow out there. And I don't know what the roads are like. I think you're just going to have to wait and see."

Chloe came to the windows and looked out. "Stupid stuff. Like we live in Canada or something."

Sarah came to stand next to her daughter. "It's kind of pretty though, don't you think? Now that the sun's out. That blue sky. The way—"

Chloe pulled away, and walked to the cupboard.

Guess my poetic descriptions were falling on deaf ears, Sarah thought.

And amazing how different the two children were. Daniel having an amazing morning piling up the snow, tunnelling. Acting like a miniature Inuit constructing his winter quarters.

And Chloe, pouring out a bowl of cereal, fretting about the

big birthday party this weekend.

But then — Sarah thought — at her age with a party ahead — she'd probably feel exactly the same way.

So, she came away from the door, went for another cup of coffee, and then sat down with her daughter.

Thinking: it's just good to be here, sitting together. Safe, warm... and as much of a family as I can make on my own.

"No boy, 'fraid you're going to have to stay here."

The snowdrifts outside would swallow Riley, and Jack planned on doing a big walk.

If the amount of snow was any indication, then Cherringham was probably "closed for business". And though he had checked in on Sarah last night, he woke up with the idea of hiking over to her place, pop in, see how they were getting on.

Guessing that there was really no need. But somehow it seemed like the thing to do.

He had to dig around for a thick scarf, and his heavy gloves... winter stuff that he really hadn't used since leaving New York.

Always was a great moment when spring seemed to finally come, and you packed away the gloves, the scarves, and the hats. Banished the shovel to the basement.

And hoped that nature had no surprises.

He checked that his phone was fully charged.

Then he went to the steps that led up to the door out of the Grey Goose, and out to the snow-covered plank.

And he began his adventurous hike.

HE GUESSED THAT there had been nearly two feet of snow. *Amazing.*

Really never thought he'd see that here. And where the wind blew, some heaves rose over three feet.

So — going was slow.

Taking a measured pace, he stepped one foot in front of the other carefully. As he trudged, he thought of the great Antarctic explorers, a subject that always fascinated him. Scott, Amundsen, the amazing Shackleton! How they faced the cold, the ice, doing exactly what he was doing here. One step at a time. Then another.

Of course, the wind here wasn't *quite* so bad. And the sun made the blizzard's aftermath look more magical than threatening.

He wanted to walk through Cherringham — that would be a sight to see. But first he'd take a dogleg around to Sarah's. *Just nip in.*

Then to the village centre. Hopefully, as he hit some of the roads he'd find ploughed areas, and walking would be easy.

He thought of calling her, alerting them... but no. Wanted this to seem casual — and not the old guy who maybe worried too much about his new friends.

When he passed the weir and crossed over the river on the bridge, he saw that the road here indeed had been recently ploughed. But already the wind had blown some of that snow back.

The main route up to Cherringham was deserted, and walking on the road reminded him of last night.

The guy he almost hit.

He wondered whether Alan had been able to learn anything. What happened, the mystery of that figure... it just wouldn't go away.

Half way up the road, he took a turn to the right to where Sarah lived. People were out shovelling in front of some of the houses. They all paused, and gave him a wave.

The camaraderie of the snowbound!

The primary school was just ahead... very quiet there with everyone on a snow day. And just a couple of roads further up, Sarah's house.

Maybe he and Daniel could do some shovelling together, he thought. Make sure there were paths to the car, the street. At least get her Rav-4 cleared of snow.

For a moment, he had the thought that maybe he was being — what would they call him in Bay Ridge? — a *nudge*.

But no. He knew Sarah too well — she'd never think that of him. And maybe, he thought, she'd have some idea this morning of where that guy came from last night.

And soon he saw her house, and could even spot Daniel in the back throwing up great shovelfuls of snow.

And didn't that look like fun...

"TIME FOR YOUR reward, boys," said Sarah, putting down the tray of tea and bacon sandwiches on the doorstep. "You know you've been out here for nearly an hour?"

She watched as Jack and Daniel leaned their shovels against the garden fence, shook the snow off their jackets, peeled off their gloves and came down the cleared path to the front door.

"No better way to get warm on a winter's day, isn't that right Daniel?" said Jack, fist bumping Daniel and getting a big grin in return.

Sarah watched her son and felt proud of him; his readiness to get stuck in. She could see that Jack too was in his element, working alongside Daniel, teaching him how to pile the snow on each side of the path ...

Like a dad, she thought.

As she looked around the front garden of her little house she was impressed by what they'd achieved.

Not just the path clear — but the pavement too, almost as far as the corner of the road. And her car — which this morning had just been a buried shape — now looked ready to go.

"Jack says if we get another dump of snow later, it'll be easier to clear now we've done this," said Daniel, reaching for a bacon sandwich.

"If?" said Jack, grabbing a sandwich too. "More a question of when, if this morning's forecast was anything to go by."

Sarah handed him his tea.

"They said just now on the radio to expect more," said Sarah.

"Brilliant!" said Daniel. "Everyone's up at Winsham Hill, Mum, can I take the toboggan?"

"If you can find it," said Sarah. "Last time I looked, it was at the back of the shed."

"Are we finished, Jack?" said Daniel.

"Sure, Daniel," said Jack. "Nice work by the way — I think your neighbours will appreciate it."

Sarah watched Daniel disappear round the side of the house in search of his toboggan, then turned back to Jack.

"First-name terms now, Jack?"

"He's a good kid. Seems crazy him calling me Mr Brennan."

"I don't see the car — did you walk up?"

"Sure. Best way to see the village, day like this."

"Must be pretty up there — I've been sorting the house all morning."

"Shut the office, huh?"

"Not worth opening," she said. "And I can do anything important on my laptop here."

"Hey," said Jack. "You can't work on a snow day!"

"I wish," she said. "But stuff'll pile up if I don't."

"So let it pile up. Hey—we could take Daniel tobogganing—"

"That'd be nice, but no way."

"Well, you're the boss. Your choice."

Sarah thought about that—and realised that it hadn't occurred to her not to work.

"But you know Sarah, another year or two and that toboggan will be at the back of the shed for good. These days don't come again. Gotta grab 'em while you can."

She looked at Jack. He was smiling at her — but underneath she could see he really meant it. She knew his daughter was grown up and gone ...

He's been there, she thought. *He's right.*

"Why not?" she said. "I might even take a turn myself. Used to be pretty good on that thing back in the day."

"Attagirl!" said Jack. "So what are we waiting for?"

"I'll get my boots."

She watched Jack grinning — and could see that this morning the retired cop had gone and standing in front of her was a New York kid with a day's adventures ahead.

5.

COMMUNITY SPIRIT

JACK WALKED DOWN Cherringham High Street with Sarah at his side, feeling on top of the world.

They'd spent a crazy couple of hours up at Winsham Hill with Daniel and his pals and he'd loved every minute. The slope was the village's traditional tobogganing run and it seemed like half the population was up there having fun.

I'm going to pay for this tomorrow, he thought.

His legs ached and his knees would not forgive him being put through that kind of punishment, clambering up snowy slopes.

But this stroll through a picture-postcard version of an English village in winter made it all seem worthwhile. The place was deserted, and in the midday sunshine he thought it looked like a scene from a Dickens story.

Magical place. Magical day, he thought.

"I thought you'd never be able to stop!" said Sarah, still laughing.

"Hey — I was in total control," said Jack. "Just I'm a little heavier than your average tobogganer — you call 'em that? — so the brakes don't quite work for me…"

"The King of Winsham Hill, Jack — you wait till I write

today up in the village magazine."

"Ouch," said Jack. "Promise you won't use the photos, huh?"

"Buy me a drink and that's a maybe—"

"Oh I see — one minute she's too busy to step out the house and now she's up for a pub crawl?"

"Lunch at the Ploughman's is what I had in mind," said Sarah. "My treat — for helping clear the snow."

Jack considered this. The pub was just a couple of hundred yards down the hill and he realised the morning's fun had left a big hole in his stomach.

"Hey, why not," he said as they drew level with the pub. "See if anyone else is out and about today — apart from the kids."

"Then tea and toast by the fire with Daniel and Chloe?"

"That's a deal, Sarah."

They kicked the snow off their boots on the old iron boot-scraper by the door to the public bar of the Ploughman's and went in.

A welcome waft of warm air and cooking smells hit Jack instantly and he knew this was a perfect idea. There was a roaring fire going in one corner and a busy clatter echoed from the kitchens behind the bar.

To his surprise, the pub was busy, tables filled and people eating.

"You know what, Jack?" said Sarah. "We're the youngest people in here."

"Well, that's something, if you're including me," said Jack.

He looked around — and indeed, it did seem like a coach-load of pensioners had been dropped off for lunch.

"What are you having Jack?" said Ellie at the bar as he approached.

"Pint of bitter."

"Spritzer please," said Sarah.

"And that smells like you got a roast on, huh?" Jack said.

"Yep, nice big joint of lamb," said Ellie. "Do you want some?"

Jack looked at Sarah who nodded.

"Yep — we definitely want," he said. "What's with the crowd, Ellie?"

"Billy's idea," she said. "He wanted to make sure some of the old people got a good hot meal. So we all came in early, got cooking."

"Good for you," said Sarah.

"He's got chains on the old Land Rover," said Ellie, "so he's just been driving around picking up the really isolated ones, bringing them in, feeding them up. Couple of the local farmers with four-wheel drives helped out too."

Jack looked around the bar. Apart from the familiar group of farmers at the locals' end of the bar chatting to Billy, the owner, he didn't recognise any of the faces. He guessed they were Cherringham old folk who lived alone; maybe had meals dropped round, carers normally looking after them.

Then he did a double take.

In one corner, he saw a familiar figure, prodding at a full plate of food. An old man in striped nightgown, but with a fleece draped round his shoulders and a blanket on his knees.

On his feet were a pair of unlaced boots, way too big for him.

He looked exactly like the ghostly apparition Jack had nearly bumped into the night before.

Same white hair, gaunt face; thin, distant gaze. Next to him, helping him eat, sat a girl he recognised who worked part-time behind the bar. Not exactly a professional carer; but she seemed to be doing her best to get the old man to eat something.

"Sarah — see the guy in the corner?" Jack said.

He watched as she followed his nod.

"If I'm not mistaken, that's the fella I nearly took out on the road down to the Goose last night."

Jack turned back to the bar.

"Ellie — the guy in the nightgown — what's the story?"

Ellie handed over his pint and topped up Sarah's wine with soda.

"He turned up last night, just before we shut," she said. "Dead lucky — another few minutes and I'd have been gone, Billy would have been upstairs with the telly on loud and matey there would have been sleeping on the doorstep."

"Sleeping?" said Jack. "I'm afraid, in that blizzard — dying more like."

"Billy brought him in, warmed him up, gave him the sofa."

"So — doesn't he want to go home?"

"That's the thing... we don't know what he wants."

"What do you mean?" said Sarah.

"He hasn't said a word since we found him."

"You don't even know who he is?"

"Nope. All we do know is — he's from the home — you know, Broadmead up past the station?"

"Ah," said Sarah.

"It's stamped on his nightshirt."

Ellie moved away down the bar to serve someone and Jack turned to Sarah: "What's Broadmead — some kind of nursing home?"

She nodded: "Private place; specialises in dementia care."

"You know it?" he said.

"Yes. You remember Beth, from the choir?"

25

Jack nodded — he sang occasionally in the village choir and Beth was one of the livelier members.

"Well, her grandmother's up at the home. I've gone visiting with her a couple of times."

"Ellie, why haven't they sent someone to pick him up?" said Jack when the barmaid returned.

"Don't know, Jack. Rang them a few times but no answer. Phone lines down maybe?"

"So what's going to happen to him?" said Jack.

Ellie shrugged. "I guess when Billy's got some time later, he'll drop him back up there in one of the Land Rovers."

Ellie was called away again to serve a customer, and Jack led Sarah to a seat by the fire.

"You seem pretty concerned, Jack," she said, sipping her drink.

Jack swallowed some of his pint and put the glass back on the table. He thought for a moment.

"Yeah — I am. I just feel it isn't right for the guy to be sitting out here without the proper people looking after him. Know what I mean?"

He watched as Sarah looked across to the old man then back again.

"And I also feel responsible. I mean - I should have searched for him longer last night, poor guy."

"You did all you could," she said. "But maybe there is something we can do now."

"How so?"

"I'm sure Billy would let us borrow the Land Rover after we've had our lunch. It would only take ten minutes for us to run the old man up to the home."

Jack nodded. *Great idea.*

"You're right. I could drop you on the way back, and then

bring the Land Rover back here."

When Billy brought over their plates of roast lamb, Jack and Sarah talked through the idea with him. Billy agreed immediately and handed the keys to Jack, then put his hands on the table and leaned in with a mock serious expression: "Just don't put it in a ditch, eh Jack?"

"Well if I do, Billy, you'll be the first to know about it," said Jack, laughing. "And I'm sure I'll never hear the end of it."

"I'll stand you a nice whisky when you're back, mate," said Billy, giving Jack a hearty slap on the back before heading back to the bar.

"You two," said Sarah.

Jack grinned at that and then tucked in to his lamb and roast potatoes.

"Eat up — we've got work to do." he said.

6.

HOME SWEET HOME

SARAH WAITED UNTIL Jack signalled that the Land Rover had heated up, then, with Ellie's help, shuffled the old man into the back seat with as many blankets as they could find.

As she and Jack drove through the deserted High Street, she realised it no longer had the chocolate box sunny charm she'd felt in the morning. To the west of the village she could see the heavy dark clouds they'd been warned about on the weather forecast.

"Look. More snow on the way, Jack," she said.

She saw Jack peer through the window at the ominous sky, then without taking his eyes off the road again: "Don't worry, we'll have you back home in an hour or two no problem. This thing will drive through anything."

Sarah looked at the frail old man wrapped up next to her and squeezed his hand tight.

So far he'd said nothing, just stared out of the windows, his pale blue eyes so sad it made her heart move for him.

"Soon have you home," she said, putting both her hands on his.

Even wrapped up as he was, his thin white hands, mottled with brown spots, were ice cold.

"THIS THE PLACE?" said Jack as they pulled up at a gated entrance.

Sarah leaned forwards and looked over his shoulder through the windscreen. Snow had piled up against the high stone walls but she could just read the words 'Broadmead Grange Nursing Home' on the snow-covered sign.

And as she peered up the long drive — deep with snow and flanked by bare oak trees — she remembered how forbidding the place had seemed when she'd been up here with her friend Beth.

"From the look of it, nobody's been in or out all day," said Jack as he gunned the engine and they crept down the drive.

They rounded a curve and the house came into view.

Dark brick, heavy stone pediments and faux battlements — like a Victorian hunting-lodge, Sarah thought.

Or a haunted castle in Transylvania...

As they pulled up by the front door, she turned to the mysterious passenger at her side. His gaze was fixed on the house.

"Look," she said, in the cheeriest voice she could conjure up. "You're home!"

He turned to her slowly, his brow furrowed, and his eyes seemed to pierce through her.

"This... isn't home," he said, speaking for the first time. "Home's a nice place."

And even in the warmth of the Land Rover, Sarah felt a chill go through her.

IT TOOK A couple of minutes of Jack banging on the front

door of Broadmead Grange before anyone came to answer.

Finally, a young woman in a nurse's uniform pulled open the door and peered at them.

"What is it you want?" she said in broken English.

Sarah remembered that last time she was here she'd noticed that nearly all the staff were from Eastern Europe.

They pay such pitiful wages, nobody from Cherringham wants the jobs, she thought.

While Jack explained that they'd found a missing patient, Sarah led the old man into the house with the nurse's help.

The nurse shut the door quickly behind them and Sarah realised how dark it was in the large hallway of the house — and also how cold.

As her eyes became accustomed to the light, she also realised that they were not alone: at various doorways that led into the central hallway, and standing at the top of the flight of stairs looking down — were old people in the familiar red-and-blue striped nightgowns but with blankets and cardigans draped around their shoulders.

She looked at Jack and could see that he'd noticed too, and was just as alarmed.

"What's going on here?" he said, gently but firmly to the young woman who'd let them in.

"What do you mean?" she said quickly. "Since the snow came, we are only three of us to look after everybody and we have no power, it is very difficult, and I am new here. You understand? We are trying very hard but it is not easy, and the emergency generator, it just — I don't know—"

Sarah could see that the woman was nearly at breaking point and knew she needed to be pretty business-like to keep her going.

"Okay, well we're here now and I'm sure we can help —

can't we Jack?"

"You bet."

"So first — this gentleman here is a patient of yours we found in the village. Why don't you help me get him back to his room?"

"And I'll see what's up with your generator."

Sarah smiled at the nurse, who nodded back.

Keep things nice and light.

"My name is Sarah — and you are?"

"I'm Ania."

"Ania," said Jack, "if you point me in the right direction I'll see if we can get some heat and light around here."

"Sure, Yes. Um, you must go through kitchens, that way, and generator is in store house at back."

Sarah put an arm around their "lost" patient then nodded to Ania: "You want to show me the way — and maybe I can help with some of the other patients, yes?"

The nurse's stiffness seemed to ease a bit at the offer of help.

"Thank you," said Ania. "Thank you very much."

The nurse led the way and Sarah nudged the old man to go with them both. Over her shoulder, she called to Jack: "Catch up with you later Jack."

So much for tea and toast by the fire back home, she thought.

JACK WENT DOWN the main corridor from the hallway, heading towards the back of the house. It was even darker down here and he pulled out his phone to use as a torch.

As he did he saw that there was no signal.

Bad sign, he thought. *Either there's just no coverage here, or the snow's taken out the local relay stations.*

This place is totally cut-off.

While he went down the corridors, he opened doors and peered in. Some of the rooms were just empty lounges, or what looked like treatment rooms or offices or storage.

He passed a few larger rooms where he guessed the residents spent their days.

He peered into one. In the gathering darkness he could barely make out what the shapes were, but as he swept the place with his light he realised it was full of old people.

They sat silently in armchairs or sofas. Some were dozing, others peered at him dopily, their arms up against the bright light.

There was a dank smell to the room that he knew so well from the last year or two looking after his elderly mother.

That had been such a sad, sad time — and the smell took him right back to those dismal days, the long visits to the home with nothing to talk about.

His own mother not recognising him, sometimes confusing him with her own long-dead father.

Jeez, that was about the lowest it ever got, he thought.

"Hi everybody," he called cheerily into the gloom. "I'm Jack and I'm here to get the lights going."

"Well get a *bloody* move on will you!" came a man's voice from one corner.

"And when you've done that you can get us a hot meal too!" came another voice.

"Bleedin' Yanks, always late to the party," said another.

Jack had to grin at that.

They may be old …

"Has he got chocolate?" came a female voice from the far side. "Love a piece of chocolate."

"Why, what are you going to give him if he has?"

"You keep your knickers on, Elsie," said another female voice and a ripple of laughter went round the room.

Amazing, Jack thought. No power, no food, no light, but these guys weren't done for by any means.

He shut the door and went further down the corridor where another door opened into the kitchens.

As he went through, his phone sweeping from side to side, he could see long lines of worktops and double cookers. The place was well kitted out and the surfaces were clean, but he caught a smell... food rotting in bins that needed be taken out.

Through the kitchens, a door opened out into a walled yard. A trail of footprints in the snow led to an outhouse. Through its window, Jack could see the flickering of an emergency light, struggling to stay lit.

What a place, he thought.

He crossed the yard and pushed open the door — immediately a bright torch light shone in his face.

"Just effing stay out of here will you!" came an angry voice from the far end of the room.

"Afraid that's not what I had in mind," said Jack, shielding his eyes. "You want to point that thing somewhere else, my friend?"

"Who the hell are you?"

"Someone who's come to help — who were you expecting?"

"I thought you was one of them bloody old zombies, I can't stop them coming in here, messing me around."

Jack crossed the room towards the torch and pointed his own light so he could see who he was talking to.

A young man in his twenties was sitting on the cement floor next to a generator, in a pile of nuts, bolts, rags and spark plugs.

Jack went over and crouched next to him.

"Well, I'm not a zombie. And I do know a little about generators. Name's Jack."

"I'm Craig."

"So Craig — you the caretaker?"

"Does it look like it? No, I'm a Healthcare Assistant, mate."

"You need a hand?"

"Too bloody right. I haven't got a clue."

"Not your line of expertise, huh, this kind of thing?"

"No way. I shouldn't even be here. I got stranded yesterday, see. First the mains power went. Then the Jenny packed up. Bleedin' nightmare it is."

Jack put down his phone, took off his jacket and rolled up his sleeves. Then he started to pick his way through the pile of parts that Craig had assembled on the concrete floor.

"What seems to be the problem?"

"It doesn't bloody work now, does it? That's the problem."

Jack took a long hard look at Craig the so-called Healthcare Assistant and took a deep breath.

It's going to be a long afternoon, he thought.

He started to sort and line up the parts, and began to draw up a checklist in his head for how he was going to diagnose and fix this generator.

Because without power, he thought, there was a real risk to the lives of the residents of this place.

Somehow they'd all have to be evacuated.

That — with another massive storm on the way.

"So what other staff are here?" he said, patiently cleaning components as he spoke.

"There's me. There's Ania — she's a nurse. And then there's the Angel of Death, of course."

"Angel of Death?"

"Sister Woods. Right bitch, she is."

"Quite the happy family then."

"Tell me about it."

"So just the three of you?"

"Yeah — three of us and about thirty zombies."

Jack put down the spark plug he was cleaning.

"Here's a thing, Craig. From now on, you're going to call the people here residents. Not zombies. Residents. Okay?"

"Yeah, maybe."

Jack kept his gaze locked on Craig. A guy like this was toxic to these old people, so vulnerable already.

"Good. That's good, Craig. Because," Jack leaned a bit closer, voice low, "if you say the word 'zombie' again I sure as hell am going to punch you into next week. Understood?"

Jack stared at Craig, his eyes not blinking. He watched as Craig seemed to fold a little, his shoulders dropping.

I think the kid got the message, he thought.

"Thanks Craig," he said. "Now let's get this thing working."

SARAH WAS ON the top floor of the nursing home, helping Ania hand out bottles of drinking water to the bed-bound residents, when the lights suddenly all came on.

She could hear muted cheers from around the building.

And as she looked across at Ania, she saw the young woman smile at her for the first time since she'd arrived.

"Ah — this is very good," said Ania. "Now the heating will work and now we can make hot food. Your friend, he is miracle worker!"

"I think I'd agree with you there, Ania," said Sarah. "Shall we get some tea on?"

The nurse nodded and Sarah followed her along the corridor, then down the stairs to the kitchens.

When she got there, Jack had already fired up a giant electric urn and was setting out teapots and milk.

He turned to her as she arrived and before she could congratulate him, he was off on a new tack:

"Can you check your phone, Sarah — you got anything?" he said urgently.

She pulled out her phone. *Nothing.*

She shook her head.

"Ania," said Jack. "You normally get phone coverage here?"

"Yes, it is always good."

"Hmm. You got a landline?"

"There is one in the office," said the young nurse.

"You show me?" said Jack to Ania, then turned to Sarah: "We need to contact the village. This place needs volunteers fast."

But before he could move, a powerful female voice boomed from the doorway.

"Volunteers? Hang on! Just what the hell's going on here?"

Sarah looked across to see a woman in her forties, in a woollen hat, thick winter jacket and boots, marching into the kitchen.

She nodded to the young nurse: "Back to work, Ania, I'll deal with this."

And Sarah watched as Ania submissively bowed her head slightly and scurried away down the corridor into the main house.

Peeling off her jacket to reveal a senior nurse's uniform, the woman now addressed Jack and Sarah: "Who the hell are you and what are you doing here?"

"Hi," said Jack. "I'm Jack Brennan, and this is a friend of mine, Sarah Edwards—"

"I *said* — what are you doing here?" repeated the woman.

"Nice to meet you, too," continued Jack. "And you are?"

"I'm Shirley Woods," she said, "Sister in charge. And you will answer me — what are you doing here?"

Sarah watched Jack smile at her.

Just the guy you want when a situation needs defusing, thought Sarah.

"Well," said Jack. "Here's the thing. We found one of your patients down in the village and it looks to me like he's been missing for nearly twenty-four hours. So I'm wondering whether you reported that fact to the police or whether there might be some issue of criminal negligence here. What with the freezing temperatures and the snow and all. What do you think, Shirley?"

"All of our patients are accounted for, I can assure you. And we do not need volunteers."

"Yeah. Um, I beg to differ, Shirley," said Jack. "Because I do not accept that without a proper staff tonight you will adequately be able to look after your residents. Am I right?"

Sarah watched Shirley: like Ania, the woman seemed at the end of her tether.

"Okay. No," she said. "You're right. In fact I just tried to get up to the village to phone head office and get help. But there's no way through. I hardly got up to the main road."

"Does your landline not work here?" said Sarah.

"Nope, that's down too," said Shirley.

Sarah watched her as she suddenly seemed to react to what Jack had said: "Hang on, did you say you brought one of our residents with you?"

"Yes," said Sarah. "He was found last night walking around the village."

"Oh, Jesus," said Shirley. "Where is he now?"

"Ania and I put him to bed in his room," said Sarah.

"And he's okay?"

"Amazingly yes," said Sarah.

"God," said Shirley. "He could have died. I'd better go see him…"

"You do that. We'll still be here," said Jack.

Sarah watched the woman go, wondering whether Shirley Woods was genuinely concerned or whether it was all for show.

"Well — she seems on the ball, at least," said Sarah.

"Wouldn't you be?" said Jack. "I suspect losing a patient is a sackable offence. Could have been charges, so damned irresponsible too, if you ask me."

Behind Jack, the urn began to boil.

"Let's get these teas sorted for everyone shall we?" she said.

She and Jack started to lay out long lines of green cups and saucers on the kitchen worktops, and Sarah went down the lines of cups, pouring milk into each.

But before Jack could follow up and pour the tea, Shirley appeared again at the door to the kitchen.

And from her face, Sarah could see that something was dreadfully wrong.

"That's not *Archy*," she said to the room. "Ania! You put him in the wrong room. That's Reg. Reg Povey."

"Sorry. This… it's not my floor. I saw the empty bed, and—"

"I don't understand," said Sarah. "You mean — there's still someone missing?"

"God. Yes," said Shirley.

"This Archy's missing — for real?" said Jack.

Shirley nodded. "Archy Fleming, yes. I just asked some of the residents. Nobody's seen him since yesterday afternoon."

"In this snow?" said Sarah.

"Unless we find him fast," said Jack. "Then he's not going to be alive."

"Jack, we'd better get back to the village," said Sarah.

"Too right," said Jack, grabbing his coat and hat.

7.

LOST AND FOUND

JACK PULLED THE Land Rover to the side of the road. Already the ploughed road had a new covering of snow, and the sky above had grown dark and thick with clouds.

He turned to Sarah on her phone, still talking to Alan who was not yet back at the police station.

"Yes. We're just going to look near the spot of Jack's accident. I know—"

She looked at Jack, nodded.

"Yes. We'll be careful. See you as soon as you get here."

She put the phone into her parka pocket.

"You sure you're up for this?" Jack said. "Might not find anything. But—"

"I'm okay," she said. "Really."

He kept his eyes on her, thinking not for the first time about how strong Sarah was.

Would have made a good cop.

"Okay, then. Let's take a look."

He popped open his door and Sarah did the same. He left the hazard warning lights on should anyone come racing down the icy road. But with blizzard part two already in progress, he guessed most people would be staying safe at home.

"I looked over that side some the other night. Maybe you want to look a bit farther there, and then I'll check this side of the road?"

He watched Sarah look around. Last night's snow made just clambering off the road a challenge.

Maybe he should do this alone.

"Sarah, the snow's really bad. Maybe I should get you back."

But she turned to him quickly. "I'm *fine*, Jack."

Yeah, he thought. *Strong.*

"Okay. I'll look over to the left, and you go a bit deeper into the woods. Alan should be here soon."

"Right," she said, and he watched her walk over to where the ploughed snow came halfway up the hedges, as she looked for a way on to the side of the road, climbing over the man-made drift.

He turned left, and they both started looking for Archy Fleming.

SARAH FOUND EACH step a challenge. One foot in front of the other was so difficult when each step sank a foot or two into snow. The fact that it had started snowing again only made it worse.

If Archy had walked this way, any tracks would have been long covered by the snow.

And as she entered the thickly wooded area, she realised that if he was following a footpath, that too would have vanished in the snow.

Now — for her — she could only guess if she was on a trail or stepping on to a jumble of rocks and branches. The snow cover made it all look the same.

Sarah glanced back — the road barely visible, Jack vanished to search the other side of the road.

She suddenly felt alone.

And with that feeling adding to the chill, she slid out her phone.

She had a signal. Not much of one, but at least she could call if needed. A lifeline out of these snowy woods to the world outside.

As she walked, she found spots where the snow was less deep, protected a bit by the overhanging branches of the few pine trees mixed with the barren deciduous trees.

The new snow still hadn't fallen so deeply in here, so maybe Archy's tracks might just be visible.

But it was getting dark. Winter, and the light vanished so early.

They wouldn't have much time before they'd have to leave.

And despite her protestations to Jack that she was... *fine...* the thought of leaving was appealing.

Get home. Ride out the second storm.

Maybe plan with Jack what they should do about the nursing home. Maybe it was something simply left to the authorities.

But meeting that nurse, the sister, all those old, vulnerable people stranded there?

And to have two of the residents slip away in the night? Without anyone even *noticing?*

Like her mentor, she had started to trust her instincts on such things.

And her instincts told her that things weren't quite all they seemed up at Broadmead Grange.

Another step — and this time she must have walked right on to a hidden boulder. The stone made her ankle twist, and she fell forwards, tumbling, arms flying out to break the fall.

And she landed on something…

At first, she didn't move.

At first — her mind suggested all sorts of benign possibilities.

She'd landed on a fallen tree trunk padded by inches of snow.

Or a pile of leaves, blown here, gathered, because—

(Because…?)

—what she'd landed on felt soft.

And as another entirely different thought occurred to her, she pulled back, recoiling, using her legs to edge backwards.

Off the tree limb.

Off the pile of leaves.

Off whatever she had fallen onto.

She took a breath as the next, most obvious thought occurred to her as she slowly stood up, trying *not* to use her hands to help in the process.

No — not wanting to press on anything with her hands. Not now that she didn't know what she would be pressing on.

The falling snow stuck to her jacket — a much wetter snow than last night, it was going to make everything so icy. Her face was dotted with small patches of the icy stuff.

Until she stood near where she'd tripped on the rock, and looked down at her landing spot.

The shape indistinct, almost unnoticed.

But she knew what it was.

The outline of a body. The head, torso, arms... legs. As if it was a snowman, lying face up in the snow, taking a rest.

And by the shape there were marks still just visible in the

snow: footprints.

Sarah could hear her steady, deep breathing. In all that she and Jack had done, she had never felt like this before.

She slid her phone out of her pocket, hoping that it still retained that single bar.

That's all I want, she thought. *Just that one bar …*

Almost afraid to look down at it.

But she did. The bar still there. Now she had to hope Jack had a signal as well.

She scrolled to his number, and pressed to call. Then up to her ear, hearing a ring which she knew didn't necessarily mean a phone was ringing anywhere.

But then:

"Yeah, Sarah?"

"Jack. Think I found him. I think—"

Words failing her.

"Okay, Sarah. Stay right there. I'll find you."

Then, ever Jack: "You okay?"

And Sarah lied. "Yeah."

She put the phone down not killing the call and hoping Jack did likewise as she waited, standing watch over the snowman at her feet.

8.

QUESTIONS IN THE WOODS

JACK CROUCHED DOWN. Sarah had watched him gently brush away snow from the top of the figure until a face was exposed.

She had to turn away from that for a moment.

Then back, as Jack performed more dusting moves, clearing more encrusted snow away from the figure. And when she did turn back, she saw the man's grey hair, frozen into spikes, sticking out at odd angles.

Eyes shut as if sleeping. And at the neck, a bit of material showing the now-familiar pattern of the nursing home's pyjamas.

Jack had called Alan, who was now only minutes away.

He turned to Sarah.

"Poor guy. Wandered in here. God knows what he was thinking."

"Probably tripped on the same rock I did."

Jack looked away, and Sarah could guess what he was thinking. Then he said it.

"I should have kept looking for him."

She touched his shoulder. "Jack, you did look, but it was

night; he could have been anywhere."

She doubted her words helped much. But in a moment, he turned to her.

"I used to tell rookie cops, when they second-guessed what they did or didn't do... you can't change the past."

"True enough."

"But what you do next, well, that's wide open."

She understood what he was talking about.

"You mean — there's something we can do now?"

"Right. That Broadmead place there. Letting this guy out, with whatever addled thinking going on, it's criminal."

"I'm sure there will be an investigation."

Jack let those words hang for a moment. She could guess how much confidence he'd have in that.

"Yeah, there will be."

She made herself look down at the body again. Who was this poor man who should have been tucked up in bed, in the warmth, watching the snow fall through a window, not wandering alone at night, lost...?

In the thick snow, she could see the trail of his footprints leading from deeper in the wood. The latest snowfall had almost filled them in, but not quite.

She tried to imagine the old man's last moments, walking through the darkness, his hands numb, grabbing at branches, stumbling, falling.

Then she saw another trail of footprints leading from the body.

She caught Jack's arm and nodded in the direction of the prints.

"Those aren't our footprints, Jack, are they?"

She watched him as he took in the extra set of prints, seeming to understand straight away why she'd asked.

"No," he said. "They're not."

"Are they his?" said Sarah. "Looks like they're going round in circles."

"Maybe he stopped here — turned around — went back and forth a bit."

"Or maybe he and Reg were here together…"

"Could be," said Jack. "Archy falls over, twists his ankle. Reg maybe goes for help?"

"Then just... ends up at the pub. Forgets about his pal."

"Funny," said Jack. "I'm thinking of them like runaways. Prisoners escaping."

"But what were they running away from?" said Sarah.

"You're right," said Jack. "Gotta wonder how bad things really were up at that home."

And at that moment, they heard a siren heading their way.

ALAN WALKED BACK with them to the road, lowering his phone

"The undertakers are sending people out. They didn't sound too happy, in this weather."

"Getting real bad out," Jack said.

"Yeah. You two best get to your homes. I'll stay out here. My job."

"Alan," Sarah said. "What will happen?"

"You mean?"

"About Broadmead. The home."

He shook his head. "Stories like this are all over the papers these days. Funds cut back. Places run on a shoestring. Things happen. And with them as short-staffed last night as you said, due to the storm…"

"Maybe nothing then?" Jack said.

The two of them walked into the holes made by their previous steps.

"I don't know, Jack. There'll be an investigation of some sort. Could be a fine maybe. But, in the grand scheme of things... You know?"

They stopped at the edge of the road, the police car parked behind the Land Rover, lights flashing, nearly dark out now.

"I will let the right people know. The police may get involved. May not. I'll talk to the staff there in the morning. Get their statements."

"Quite the crew," Jack said.

"I can imagine."

"What about the people there now? Maybe even relatives of people we know in the village. They going to be okay?"

"You guys got the generator going. There's heat, food. Not much more I can do, at least tonight. 'Cept, deal with the man back there."

"Archy," Jack said.

"Hmm?"

"His name's Archy. Who knows what his life was like. And it ends like this."

Sarah realised that Jack had been thinking about the old man's sad death too. She looked at Alan's face to see if Jack's words stung.

"Right, I know Jack. We'll all do our best. Going to be a busy night out here."

Which is when Jack took a step closer to Alan. And Sarah thought, this must be how he talked to his rookies on the NYPD.

He put an arm on Alan's shoulder. "I know you will but... we had a question. Would you mind, when the storm ends, if we do a little talking? To the people in the home. To those who work there."

Alan took a second, thinking about it.

Then: "Don't see why not. You brought one of their people back, helped them get power. Some friendly follow-up makes sense to me. After all, this isn't a police matter."

Jack nodded. Then: "Not yet."

And with that Sarah looked up — the damn snow still falling.

"We'd better go, get the Land Rover back."

"Right," Alan said.

And she and Jack walked on to the road, already with an inch-thick covering.

It was going to be a long night indeed.

THE PLOUGHMAN WAS — amazingly enough — still full. But not with old folk any more. Sarah recognised a few faces: some of the pub's stalwarts had made it through the snow. One day of cabin fever seemed to be the most the regulars could take.

Though Sarah guessed that Billy would soon shoo them away and close the place.

He had asked how things went, and she and Jack shared with him about finding Archy — and at the same time, asked him to keep it quiet.

If she and Jack were going to start asking questions about Broadmead, it was better if people didn't know what had happened last night.

"Love to stay for a drink," she sad to Jack, "but I'd better be heading back—"

"Walk you home."

"No, it's out of your way. It will be okay. You've got the

big trudge, back to the Goose."

"Looking forward to getting there."

They reached the door, the flakes flying around in the bright pools made by the pub's outdoor lighting.

"I'm going to try and get into the office first thing in the morning. Got a ton of work to do. But I'll do some digging as well. On the home, see if I can find out who owns the place. Whether it's had any investigations for bad care."

"Great. I'm guessing that this isn't the first time."

"And maybe who works there. Think they're supposed to go through a security check — I'll dig around."

"Then we head back there, yes?"

"Even if we have to walk it, Jack."

Jack opened the door. "Good for you." She saw Jack look up to the illuminated flakes spinning down. "Cherringham in winter. More like upstate New York. Stay safe."

And Sarah smiled then hurried out to the road as they both headed home.

9.

SECRETS OF BROADMEAD GRANGE

WHEN SARAH WOKE next morning and peered out of her bedroom window she could see it had snowed all night again: her Rav-4 was buried under a huge drift. Taking another day off wasn't an option — she knew she had to get in to work.

The downside of running your own business, she thought.

Leaving the kids in bed, she grabbed a quick coffee, then put her head down against the blizzard and trudged up through the estate and into the village square.

The centre of Cherringham was silent and empty. The few cars that had been left in the car park were almost hidden in snowdrifts.

When she got to her office door, it was a relief to find her assistant Grace just ahead of her, with two coffees and a couple of croissants from the local café.

"You're joking," said Sarah. "Huffington's is open, in this?"

"Place has never closed," said Grace. "At least — not in my lifetime!"

After they'd caught up with each other's news, Sarah got stuck into some revised copy and images for the upcoming Walk for Mental Illness brochures. She knew the group had limited funds and so she did it for cost only. A website make-over for Howie's Turkey Farm would more than cover any loss.

Then — into the background of Broadmead.

She quickly found that it was operated by Hearthstone Investments. But beyond that, there seemed to be no information.

While Sarah knew that she was supposed to be the expert on all things internet, she called over Grace, who grew savvier by the week.

"Grace — I'm getting a listing for the company that owns that home. But no names, no contacts. All there is is a generic-sounding email."

Grace slid over to Sarah's desk on her wheeled chair.

"Hmm. Must be a private concern. I think there are different regulations regarding names, disclosure... for that versus a public company, aren't there?"

"Maybe. But usually you can at least get a name. It's as if whoever is running Hearthstone — and Broadmead — doesn't want to be known."

"Based on what you told me about the place, I'm not surprised."

Sarah sat back, for the moment stymied.

Then Grace leaned forward and tapped the screen. "Maybe we should work backwards?"

"Hmm?"

"Start with the home, any trails that lead to it on the net. Reports, or maybe they had some work to be done, something needing approval? See if that leads to Hearthstone... and maybe a name."

"Brilliant. You should be running this place."

"Learning from the best, Sarah," Grace said, sailing back

to her own desk, and hi-res images of turkeys looking eager and happy to meet their maker.

And Sarah did as Grace suggested.

NOT MUCH POPPED UP, but then — from just a few months back — a report of a break-in. No loss reported, but the owner — Hearthstone — contacted, and a name behind that... Richard Leacock.

It rang a bell.

Searching it, she found that he had an office in the nearby village of Brampton.

Cute village. Even more upmarket than Cherringham. Property prices through the roof.

Leacock was clearly doing a good job keeping his name distant from the nursing home his investment company ran.

She was tempted to call him but thought she... *they...* might get only one shot at that, so best to wait until she and Jack knew more.

Then — to the website for the Care Quality Commission — the regulator for Care Homes. The euphemistically bland government body also had a suitably vague and maze-like site. Hard to find where one could find a record of any investigations and charges.

Who designs these things? she thought.

Like they're hiding Easter eggs.

But after going back and forth from the main page to the various off-shoots, she finally found a page that linked to past investigations, and establishments that had been investigated.

She scrolled down the list.

And came to the name 'Broadmead'.

She wanted to call Jack — but before she could, her phone

trilled.

Beth Travers.

And Sarah took the call from her good friend and discovered that — even in a blizzard — word travels fast.

JACK WATCHED RILEY attempt to bound through the snow, flopping ahead a few feet then racing back to his previous position as if the white stuff was an enemy to be faced.

Then, to the right, coming over the narrow bridge by the weir, he saw Sarah's car, moving slowly.

So the road had been ploughed. In the night, Jack thought he'd heard the teams at work. She'd have to park well away from the mooring of the Goose and trek over.

But a cup of coffee and some planning before they went back to Broadmead would be good.

He watched as Sarah began walking along the river edge, the snow less deep there, to where Jack stood outside, a steaming cup of coffee in his hand.

"Morning. Roads all good?"

"Some. Amazingly the old Rav started. Think it may be quite a while before your little Sprite gets out."

Jack laughed at that. "That's okay. Going to be a pedestrian for a while. Kids have another day off?"

"God, yes. They're over the moon. Two snow days in a row! They feel like American kids. Never happens."

Riley came bounding back and went over to say hello to Sarah.

"Hello boy!" then to Jack, "Seems like Riley loves the stuff too."

"Does, doesn't it?" Then: "Come on in. Have a coffee, and... I think I have those biscuits you like."

"Great."

And she followed Jack on to the deck of the Goose, then down to the small galley.

JACK TOPPED HIS coffee off as Sarah took a sip.

"You do like it strong, don't you?" she said.

"'Fraid so. Want to ditch it for some tea?"

"No. Perfect. All that caffeine! Feel more awake already. So let me tell you about Beth."

"Nice woman."

"The best, and she had heard about what happened with Archy and Reg. She even knew about the power failure. Her grandmother's there, Jack. Odelia Travers. Ninety-two years young."

"Wow. Some name. And some age."

"Heart of gold, too. I knew her well when I was younger. Pillar of Cherringham."

"I bet."

"And Beth's parents are living in Catalonia, thinking everything is okay. Beth says she doesn't get to see her grandmother as often as she'd like — but this has her concerned."

"Hence the call, huh?"

"She asked if we were going to look into things."

"Hope you told her most definitely. And not just for Odelia. That building is filled with hard-working people who raised families. Probably war heroes as well."

Jack took a breath. Things like this got to him.

"Told her we were going there today. We'd check on Odelia."

"Good. And if Miss Woods doesn't like our dropping in we can say we were asked by a relative."

"Perfect."

Then Sarah told him about her discovery of the owner of the place.

"Brampton. Nice village. You know it?"

"*Very* upscale," said Jack. "Guessing this Leacock is doing well running the home?"

"Doing well, if you don't count the loss of a resident or two."

Jack finished his coffee. "And this investigation you found," he said, "No charges?"

"No." She pointed out a line on the printout she'd made. "But see here... it says 'warning issued'. About 'general conditions'."

"Guessing that's food, living quarters, rats in the basement?"

"Who knows? Couldn't find out anything else. Guess we might dig up more at the home."

"Yeah. I wonder... did things change after that report? Get better, get worse? Has there been any follow-up?"

"That's all they had on the website," Sarah said.

Jack nodded. "Bet it's another case of a government agency overwhelmed. From what I saw, the 'general conditions' of the place were none too good."

Sarah took one of the shortbread-like biscuits, and dipped it in her coffee.

"Imagine there will be an investigation now, what with Archy escaping."

"Funny," Jack said. "That word... 'escaping'."

"You think it got so bad that—?"

"Don't know what to think, but — on behalf of Odelia and everyone else stuck there — let's hope we find out."

Riley, sitting by the door, made a grumbling noise.

"I think he wants to go out and play some more."

"Guess dogs are like kids. They love the snow."

Sarah stood up. "Wish I could say the same. Ready to head out?"

"Sure. Just a word of caution—"

"What's that?"

"When we get there... they may not have told the other residents about Archy yet."

"Oh, right."

"Could be pretty frightening for them. Perhaps some of them were his friends."

"Got it."

Jack pulled on his parka, and cloth cap tight, and after putting their cups in the sink, walked to the stairs up and out of the Goose.

But then he turned to Sarah.

"And you know, for anyone living there, I'd say you'd have good reason to be frightened."

And they left the boat for the snowy way back to Sarah's car.

10.

NO PLACE LIKE A HOME

SHIRLEY WOODS OPENED the door, and Sarah saw that whatever scowl she had worn previously instantly deepened at the sight of the two of them.

"God, now what the — what are you two doing back here?"

Jack, ever the diplomat when it came to potentially criminal situations, took a step closer.

"Sister Woods, we're actually here to check up on—" he shot Sarah a glance, "an old family friend, Odelia Travers."

"She's fine. They're all *fine*, and anyway, visiting hours are over—"

"Except," Jack said, "for Archy Fleming."

Wow, Sarah thought.

Jack does know how to play his cards.

And that stopped the home's senior nurse. Then:

"Like I told the police — he was... confused. Not thinking straight. I — we can't—"

"You know it was us who found him?" Sarah added, as if trying to give more reasons why they should come in and check on Odelia.

Then Sarah added, "Actually, *I* found him. Face up, in the

snow. And for Odelia, for the others, we'd just like to help."

Better to use the word "help" than the more ominous *find out what the hell is going on*, Sarah guessed.

A nod from the formidable Shirley Woods, and the giant door of the place slowly opened.

But before they went in she caught Jack give her a look, a smile... and Sarah realised that when it came to card-playing, she wasn't exactly without skills herself.

THEY FOUND ODELIA Travers sitting in a corner of a large common room. A muted TV off to one side ran a sitcom with grinning teenagers. Other residents sat quietly at tables or on sofas, some knitting, some dozing, no one looking at the screen.

"There she is," Shirley Woods said.

Sarah noticed the sister softening a bit. "She's quite a girl. Even at her age, has a smile for everyone."

"Thanks," Sarah said.

Then: "You can see she, the others... all of them, are perfectly fine."

Shirley Woods walked away. And Sarah, taking the lead, walked over to Odelia. Jack stayed back a bit.

The old woman looked so tiny; sitting all bundled up by the window, looking out at the snow, now glistening in sunlight. She had a napkin between her gnarled fingers that had been twisted and turned, shredding.

"Mrs. Travers?" Sarah said quietly.

The woman turned away from the window, her face immediately confused. Sarah looked at Jack. A small nod there.

"Mrs. Travers, how are you? It's me, Sarah Edwards."

Then, like a light switch coming on, the old woman's face brightened, eyes widening. "Sarah, my Beth's Sarah, yes?"

Now it was Sarah's turn to smile. "Yes, it is. Glad you remembered."

"You two," she kept grinning, "as thick as thieves. I seem to remember that you liked those little muffins I used to bake."

Sarah laughed. "You bet I did. Raisins, butter…"

"Piping hot!" the woman said, looking away as if she could picture herself pulling a tray of muffins out of the oven for her granddaughter and her best friend.

"Mrs. Travers, I was wondering if we could talk to you a bit?"

Only now did Odelia take in Jack, standing a few feet to the side.

Odelia's smile faded a bit. "Talk?"

"Beth asked me to drop by, what with the big storm and everything. And my friend Jack here offered to come along."

Odelia appeared to think about this for a moment. Then:

"Well, of course. Have a seat you two. If this place wasn't so understaffed, I'd see if they could manage some tea." She lowered her voice. "No chance of that happening."

Sarah pulled a straight-backed chair from a nearby card table close to Odelia, Jack as well. And they sat in the sun streaming from the window, the snowy piles just on the other side of the glass.

"OH, I'M *FINE*. Place has got, well, a bit run down these last few months. You can see that. But they feed me; make sure I'm all right at night. They could be nicer about it, though …"

Jack cleared his voice. "Mrs. Travers, does it seem like everyone's being taken care of okay?"

"Everyone? Hmm," Then she stopped. "You're an *American*, aren't you?"

Jack laughed. "Why, yes I am."

A big smile from Odelia. "Always liked Americans." Then a look to Sarah. "You two, the two of you, aren't—?

Now Sarah's turn to laugh "No. Just good friends."

She left out any of the detective stuff. This Odelia seemed sharp enough that she could easily put two and two together, and sense that something was wrong here... that something had happened.

In fact — she might well do that anyway.

"Well, to your question, Jack. I have heard people complain. Not getting medications on time, left in bed all day. Me, I'm pretty independent. But such things wouldn't surprise me. And since these big storms, well, it's a skeleton crew here, I can tell you."

Jack nodded. "Big storms," Jack said. "They really hit the village." Sarah noticed that he looked at her, maybe unsure about his next question.

"Do you know a resident here... Archy Fleming?"

"Archy! Everyone here knows old Archy." Again, Odelia leaned close. Her voice was already a croaky whisper but she lowered it even more. "Crazy old sod. But the tales he can tell."

Sarah picked up on that: "Gets a bit confused, does he?"

"A bit? Half the time he doesn't know where in the world he is. Sometimes cruising the Adriatic, other times ready to meet the Queen."

That had Odelia laughing. Another twist of the paper napkin between her fingers. "But he's such a sweet, sweet man... even with most of the marbles out of his jar."

Jack laughed. "Sounds like you like him?"

"Oh yes, we all do. Funny old Archy. Haven't seen him this morning though."

Keeping it quiet here, Sarah guessed.

And something lingered in Sarah's mind with that. Not quite sure what it was... more instincts, a feeling?

Something here.

"And I guess you know Reg Povey?"

"Reg? Yes, new here. Can't say I know him as well as old Archy."

Sarah nodded: "But equally as, um, confused?"

Again, Odelia didn't seem to understand that question.

"Reg? Haven't spoken to him much. Like I say, he's new here."

Jack pulled his chair a bit closer.

"Odelia, you've been here a while, hmm?" he said.

"Oh, yes. Not the best place, probably not the worst."

"Can you think of any reason why anyone would want to hurt Archy or Reg?"

As if on cue, Sarah heard a voice booming behind them, a man in a blue tartan robe, fluffy slippers.

"Morning prayers in the main chapel, eight a.m. sharp!"

Sarah saw who it was …

Reg Povey.

Talk about timing!

"There he is," Odelia said, sounding relieved. "Hurt him, or Archy? Why on earth would anyone want anything to happen to those two old coots?"

She shook her head at this.

But Sarah guessed some wheels were spinning in Odelia's mind. "And, and there he is, fit as a fiddle." A small smile returned. "Though what chapel he's talking about, I have no idea. Still — like my husband Arnold used to say... 'whatever floats your boat'."

"See you all in the chapel promptly," Reg announced.

Then he turned to leave the room — but not before glancing over at Jack and Sarah.

Perhaps espying new parishioners for his non-existent church.

But — Sarah thought — he held that look, as if he was about to come over.

Then, in his dementia, or whatever he had, he instead made the sign of the cross, blessing all the souls in the common room and left.

And when she turned back to Odelia, she had also, in kind of a way, *left*. Staring out the window, gazing at the snow.

Maybe thinking of the countless snowfalls in her lifetime.

It all goes so fast, Sarah thought. *I need to remember that.*

She reached out and covered Odelia's intertwined hands.

"We'll leave you for now, hmm?"

Odelia nodded.

"But is it okay if we pop around, visit from time to time?" Jack said. And Sarah knew he meant it.

"I — I'd like that," Odelia said.

Sarah gave those hands a squeeze. "Later then."

And they got up.

OUT IN THE hallway they ran into Ania, arms full of bed sheets.

"Ania!" Sarah said.

The nurse still seemed tentative, guarded.

"Are you still short-staffed because of the storm?"

"Me, changing beds? You could say that." The nurse looked eager to hurry on, but Sarah had one quick question.

"Ania, can you tell me where the chapel is?"

"The chapel? Yes, it is through the common room — that way."

She pointed across the hallway to a corridor, then hurried away.

Sarah turned to Jack.

"Why don't I look in on the morning service, while you see if you can track down our favourite member of staff?"

"Nothing would give me greater pleasure," said Jack.

Sarah watched him turn and head towards the office.

Would she get any sense out of Reg?

11.

SUSPECTS

SARAH PUSHED OPEN the door to the chapel and peered into the darkened room.

As her eyes adjusted, she realised, looking around, that what must at one time have been a Christian place of worship had been converted into a multi-faith room of prayer.

No crosses, statues, stained glass. Just white walls, simple chairs, pictures of trees and flowers.

Like being in one of those airport prayer rooms, she thought.

She spotted Reg, sitting on a chair in a dark corner, his fluffy slippers out of place in this austere setting.

She went over and sat next to him. At first, he didn't react to her presence — but then he slowly turned and stared straight at her, his eyes seeming to search her face for clues.

"Did we have dinner?" he said. "Is it bedtime?" He didn't seem to recognise her from the previous day.

"No, Reg. It's not bedtime, not yet," said Sarah.

She smiled at him and he nodded; his face serious.

Did he understand? His face, his eyes, seemed alert even if his words didn't make much sense.

"I'm not hungry anyway," he said. "Padre will be here soon."

"That's good, Reg. Do you like it in here?"

"You pays your money, you takes your choice," he said.

Sarah realised she didn't have the skills or experience to deal with someone in Reg's condition. But she desperately wanted to find out if he knew anything, even the slightest detail about what had happened on the night Archy had died.

"Reg — can you remember what happened to Archy?"

She saw Reg's eyes light up.

"Archy's my mate."

"I know."

She watched as Reg's sombre face suddenly broke into a cheeky grin.

"He's a proper ladies' man, Archy is. Wanna watch yourself with him, sweetheart!"

"I will," she said, smiling at Reg. "Reg — do you remember going in the snow with Archy?"

"Bloody cold that was," said Reg. "Caught my death."

"Why did you go out in the snow?"

"Saw the chance — took it!"

"What happened out in the woods? Do you remember?"

"Guards caught us, brought us back. Next time, eh?"

He leaned across and put his mouth close to her ear. Sarah could smell his breath, stale, and — incongruously — a pungent odour of cheap aftershave: "Word is — there's a tunnel on the go."

He tapped his nose — Sarah nodded back to him as if she knew it must be kept secret.

"So, were you trying to escape, Reg?"

"Been here bleedin' years, got to get out."

"Don't you like it here?"

The old man suddenly grabbed her arm, his hand tight.

"Can you get me out? Can you? I'll pay you! I've got

millions! I have!"

"I'm sorry Reg, I can't really do anything," said Sarah, feeling totally powerless. "Maybe if you—"

But Reg got up suddenly and pushed his chair back. Without another glance at her, he stepped over her legs and headed for the door.

She watched, bemused, as he pulled open the door. Then he turned and clapped his hands together, the sound echoing in the little chapel.

"Come on! Chop chop! Mess dinner tonight!"

She watched him scan the room.

"No takers? Your loss mateys, your loss!"

And then he was gone.

Sarah wasn't sure she'd learned anything new. But she knew one thing — she and Jack had been right to use the word 'escape'. Archy and Reg had certainly been escaping — but from what?

JACK PEERED AT the grainy CCTV footage and used the remote to fast-forward. The screen, split in four, showed different angles of the exterior of Broadmead Grange.

Four different shots of snow falling, thought Jack. *Some hope.*

"You're lucky we've still got that, you know," said Shirley, placing a chipped mug of tea on the office table next to him. "If it hadn't been for the power cut, it would have been recorded over by now."

Jack didn't take his eyes off the monitor, but he was aware that the sister had taken her seat at the other side of the desk and was watching over his shoulder.

"Appreciate you letting me see it," he said.

"Like I told you — we don't have anything to hide," said

Shirley.

"Right. And I just want to be sure in my own mind that none of your staff is responsible for the death of that old man."

"Judge and jury, are you?"

"We have a friend here in the home — just looking after her interests."

"Don't think I don't know who you and your friend are, Mr. Brennan. Cherringham's own private detectives. I just wonder who's paying you. And whether I should tell my boss what you're up to."

"Tell who you like," said Jack. "Nice tea, by the way — thank you."

"You're welcome."

Jack looked at the time code in the top corner of the screen. Still only five p.m. on the evening Archy and Reg fled into the snow.

On the screen he saw the front door to the home suddenly open. He paused the tape and hit the play button.

In the grainy playback, he could see a stream of people in coats and hats emerging from the Home — some on their own, some in small groups. With their heads down against the blizzard, they headed out of frame.

"Lot of people leaving," said Jack.

"Five p.m. shift finishing. That's them heading up to catch the twenty-past train," said Shirley.

"Very noble of them to leave just as the blizzard was coming in," said Jack, speeding up the tape and watching the figures scuttle away from the building.

"How noble would you be on minimum wage, Mr. Brennan, with your family at home waiting for you?"

"Touché," said Jack.

"Besides — the night shift were due in on the next train."

"Except they never turned up, did they? So where's your emergency cover huh?"

"We didn't expect to be snowed in, so we didn't hire any."

"You don't say? Nobody listens to the weather forecasts huh? Or did Mr. Leacock refuse to pay for extra help?"

Jack waited for the sister to respond, but her silence gave him the answer anyway.

"I'm looking forward to meeting Mr. Leacock, by the way," he said.

Again, no answer. He watched the time code whizz onwards, now six p.m., now seven...

"I hear the home got into trouble with the authorities last year. Guess you were in charge then?"

"The problem was just in the kitchens," said Shirley. "I'm only responsible for patient care."

"Not responsible? Where did I ever hear that line before?"

"My staff do a difficult job for very little money and even less thanks, Mr. Brennan. I don't care for your moralising."

"Just calling it as I see it," said Jack, still not taking his eyes off the screen.

Time to change tack, he thought.

"What's the security routine at night?"

"After supper, residents get a hot drink and the nurses administer whatever routine medication is prescribed where appropriate. Then lights out—"

"Doors locked?"

"Of course — the building is secured and the night staff monitor until morning."

"No CCTV inside the building?"

"Regular room visits from the care assistants has always been adequate. If a patient presses the help button we respond."

"But if a patient got up and left the building you'd be none the wiser."

"We'd see them on the security monitor, here in the office."

"But you didn't, did you?"

"Because instead of having six staff that night we only had three," said Shirley.

Clearly not happy with these questions.

"You, Ania and the charming Craig — that right?"

Jack looked over his shoulder quickly at Shirley. She nodded to him, but clearly wasn't going to be drawn into a conversation about her staff.

Jack turned back to the monitors and saw a blur of movement in the shot of the back door and courtyard.

"Speak of the devil," he said. "Isn't that Craig there?"

He rewound the tape and played it back slowly. The time-code read nine p.m. He leaned forward and concentrated on the quarter image on the screen. The top-down view made it hard to see faces clearly and the lens was already partly covered in snow.

But Jack was sure that the figure was Craig.

The care assistant had pushed open the exterior door and stood in the shelter of the porch smoking a cigarette.

Then Jack saw him turn and talk to someone in the doorway.

"You got no other angle on this?" he said to the sister. "Who's he talking to?"

"This is all there is," said Shirley. "It must be Ania, the nurse."

"Could be you," said Jack.

Jack peered at the screen. Craig reached into his pocket and handed the mysterious figure a cigarette, then appeared to light it for them.

"I don't smoke, Mr. Brennan," said Shirley.

So maybe it is the young nurse, thought Jack.

But his instincts said the other smoker was a male. Something about the way they stood, moved…

Jack watched for ten minutes, but not once did the mystery figure emerge clearly. All he could see was a shape in the doorway. Finally, Craig flicked his butt-end away and the two smokers slipped back into the building.

"See the door?" said Jack. "He didn't shut it properly. Archy and Reg could have easily slipped out that way."

"People aren't perfect," said Shirley. "Anyone can make a mistake."

"Even a fatal mistake?" said Jack.

He fast forwarded again — and sure enough, just twenty minutes later into the tape, the door swung open and he saw a man in a robe and pyjamas walk out into the billowing snow.

"That's Archy," said Shirley, over his shoulder.

Jack heard a slight tremble in her voice. Maybe the sister wasn't quite as tough as she made out?

It was chilling to see the old man, in just slippers and a flimsy robe standing in the blizzard.

Jack watched carefully, straining to interpret what he was seeing in the grainy, snow-blown images. There had to be clues in here. Had to be…

Archy shifted right and left, looking lost and confused in the courtyard. He then turned back to the door as if he might go in again.

But then he started talking — Jack could just see his mouth moving rapidly.

Who was he talking to?

Jack watched the tape: another resident now stepped out

of the doorway into the courtyard. The camera now gave a full view of both men.

"Reg," he said.

He saw Reg catch up with Archy and talk briefly.

Then the two old men just walked off together, disappearing from the frame.

Jack looked at the time on the clock — nine-thirty. He'd had his accident at around ten p.m. Just time for them to walk through the snow into the village. It all made sense.

He turned away from the monitor. He knew the two residents wouldn't be coming back into shot.

Ever.

He looked at Shirley. She was still staring at the monitor.

"Where were you at nine-thirty that night Shirley?" said Jack.

"I, er—" She hesitated. Seeing the escape had obviously rattled her. "Um, up on the top floor, looking after a ninety-eight-year-old lady who was having a panic attack," she said. "S-so don't tell me I should have been here looking at these damned screens. Don't you tell me I'm responsible for Archy's death."

Jack could see that in spite of her protest, Shirley Woods *did* feel responsible.

But he also felt that she shouldn't. Tough she might be — but from what he'd seen, maybe this woman was the only thing holding the whole place together.

And the real guilt lay elsewhere.

He got up.

"I get that, Shirley. Lot of people here needing help that night."

"Yes."

"Least now we know how they got out." Jack stood up.

"Thanks for the tea," he said. "I know it hasn't been easy, but you've been helpful."

He watched as she put his mug in a small sink, then went to the door and opened it wide for him to leave.

"That may be. But I'd rather you didn't waste any more of my time or that of my staff, Mr Brennan," she said. "I've still only got half my rota back on duty and whatever you may think, I do care about the residents here."

Jack nodded as he left, and said nothing.

But as walked down the long dark corridor towards the front door, the image of Archy standing bewildered in the thick snow of the courtyard wouldn't go away.

Whoever was responsible for his death wasn't going to get away with it.

SARAH STOOD IN the hallway putting on her coat, and watched Jack walking grimly down the long corridor towards her. She'd spent the last half hour talking to some of the other patients. Residents? Was that the word she should use?

Or prisoners?

And now she wanted out. The building felt too grim and soulless to bear any longer. And now they'd got full power back on, the neon lights in the high ceilings just served to show how Spartan the whole place was.

She handed Jack his coat and hat as he reached her.

"You find Reg?" he said.

She nodded.

"No use, huh?"

"He remembers he was trying to escape and that's about it," she said. "How about you?"

Before he could answer, Ania and Craig emerged through

a door at the side, pushing a small trolley. Sarah realised that she and Jack were in their way, and moved to one side — but she saw Jack not budging.

Something's happened, she thought.

"Well," said Jack. "If it isn't my favourite Healthcare Assistant. That's what you are, Craig, isn't it?"

"Please, we have to make the drugs round," said Ania, looking frightened by the situation.

"I've just been watching you on TV, Craig," said Jack.

Sarah could see Craig's eyes flicking from her to Jack to Ania. He's nervous, she thought.

Craig licked his lips.

"Oh yeah?" said Craig. "Can't have been me. No bloody way!"

"Oh, it was," said Jack. "CCTV footage from the other night."

Sarah watched Jack, confident, knowing — and then looked at Craig, thirty years his junior probably, but clearly scared. Even in the cold hallway, she could see beads of sweat forming under his lank hair.

He looks guilty as hell, she thought. *But guilty of what?*

"You just let us through now," said Craig with an artificial grin that nearly made Sarah laugh out loud. "You see, we... we, er — got patients to look after."

"Really?" said Jack. "I've seen the way you look after patients, Craig. Give them cigarettes—"

"That's not a crime, letting 'em have a fag now and then."

"Maybe not. But selling them cigarettes, that's gotta be, no?"

"No way, and look, they can smoke outside if they want; it's not a prison—"

"Outside, sure. But in a freezing blizzard?" said Jack.

"Interesting take on the notion of 'care' there, Craig. And leaving doors open so the residents can just walk out and die in the snow — that part of your job description too?"

Sarah watched Craig's eyes go wide, like he was trapped. For a second she thought he was going to throw a punch at Jack.

That would have been interesting to see.

Jack would see it coming from a mile away.

But Craig obviously thought better of the idea and transferred his energy to the drugs trolley, pushing it hard towards Jack's legs to get by.

"Just get the hell out the way, will you?" said Craig, as he shot off down the corridor. Then he called over his shoulder: "Ania, get your arse down here, I can't do this on my own."

Sarah gently reached out a hand towards Ania, but the young nurse pulled back, offered a muttered "sorry" and then caught up to Craig.

"Poor girl," said Sarah, watching Ania disappear. She turned to Jack: "What was that all about, Jack?"

"I have an idea. Tell you in the car," said Jack, putting on his coat. "You know, the only thing that surprises me about this place is that it survived its last inspection. House of Horrors. Come on, let's go. I can't stand another minute here."

"Me neither," said Sarah.

She pulled open the front door and they went out into the never-ending blizzard; into the clean, white, snowy landscape.

12.

TEA FOR TWO

A GUY COULD get used to this, thought Jack, settling back into the deep sofa and stretching his legs closer to the open fire.

Richard Leacock's house had been hard to find — especially in the snow — but Jack had finally pulled up in front of the eighteenth-century mansion in his little Sprite and he had to admire Leacock's taste.

What would the Cherringham real estate experts call the house, with its tall curved ground-floor windows, wisteria growing around the front door, fountains, weeping willows?

Charming, discreet, refined, elegant …

Hey, the guy even had a butler.

Now that *I gotta write home about,* thought Jack.

Not in a coat and tails, but nevertheless — a real live butler.

He poured himself another coffee from the little cafetiere on the table by the sofa and popped another almond biscuit into his mouth.

Very comfortable.

And all of it created out of the exploitation of vulnerable old folk and hard-pressed carers and nurses.

He checked his watch — he'd been here twenty minutes and still no sign of the man himself, apart from an apology from the butler and an instruction to make himself comfortable.

As if on cue, the door opened and Jack readied himself to meet the mysterious owner of Broadmead Grange.

"Mr. Brennan, I am *so* sorry to have kept you."

Jack stood up and took in the man walking towards him.

Leacock was tall, greying, in a checked shirt and maroon v-neck jumper. A broad smile, warm eyes and a firm handshake — followed by a sociable pat on the shoulder.

"Unforgivable of me. Conference call, I'm afraid, simply had to take it. Would you like more coffee? Wonderful biscuits, aren't they? Home-made, right here in our kitchen, cook's a marvel."

Jack watched as Leacock settled himself into an armchair by the fire and gestured for him to sit back in the sofa too.

"I can't tell you how glad I am to see you, Mr Brennan," said Leacock.

"Oh really?"

"Absolutely. I assume you are here to talk about Broadmead?"

"Broadmead, yes. And the death of Archy Fleming."

"Mr Fleming, yes, of course. God. Terrible. Tragic. Awful. We were all so upset to hear about that."

"I bet."

Jack watched Richard Leacock as he finally picked up on Jack's attitude.

A little light bulb going off.

"Mr Brennan, am I right in thinking that you hold me — or perhaps my company — in some way *accountable* for the desperately sad events of the last few days?"

Jack shrugged.

"You're the boss of Hearthstone. Hearthstone owns

Broadmead. Broadmead is so badly staffed and resourced that a vulnerable old man was allowed to leave the house in the middle of a blizzard, and his absence was only noticed when police reported they'd found his body." Jack shook his head. "And you *don't* feel responsible, Mr Leacock?"

"I feel desperately sorry, of course. And angry about the death—"

"But not responsible?"

Jack watched Leacock get up from the sofa and walk to the windows, where he stood for a few seconds, then turned.

"I hadn't expected you to be so hostile, Mr Brennan."

"Are you kidding me? You living up here, like this — and the people in that home in the cold, the dark, no heating, no light…"

"I had no idea — no one told me that they lost power. I pay people—"

"Pay them a ton, do you?"

Again, Leacock stopped. "I did not know."

"You know, if I hear that one more time — 'had no idea', 'not my responsibility'."

Jack was getting angry. He wanted to deck the guy, right here in his cosy living room.

Instead, he took a breath. Anger would not be helpful.

"Okay, Mr Leacock, you said you were glad to see me. Now why would that be?"

Jack watched Leacock as he walked back to the armchair and sat down.

"Well, to be honest, I thought you were here to help me."

"Why the hell should I *help* you?"

"Perhaps if I explain the… architecture… of all this, it might be clearer?"

"Go ahead, I'm listening."

"I own Hearthstone — right? Or rather, there's a trust in my name which owns Hearthstone."

"In the Cayman Islands, let me guess."

"Channel Islands, actually, but yes. Anyway that's a side issue. So, Hearthstone has a portfolio of investments and one family of those is healthcare — expanding sector you know, very good yields — and a small part of that family is Broadmead Grange."

Leacock now sounded like he was sitting in a board meeting somewhere, rattling off information.

"Broadmead is one of ten homes across the UK all owned and run by Broadmead Enterprises which has its own management structure, or rather it did until half way through last year when the homes were split into two smaller groups under different management teams—"

"Whoa, whoa, whoa — Mr. Leacock, you're losing me with the 'who owns what'. Just what is your point?"

"Sorry, sorry. Okay, here's the point. Theoretically, I own Broadmead. But I have no involvement. I've never even *been* there. There's supposed to be a management team — but half of them were asked to resign about six months ago and apparently they've not been replaced."

"So you're telling me that nobody's running the place?"

"As far as I know, the senior nurse—"

"Shirley Woods?"

"Yes, that's her. Though apparently she is also taking legal action against Broadmead on various counts."

"What? The person running things is suing the people who own it?"

"That's what I hear from the board of Broadmead."

"She didn't tell me that."

"I'm not surprised. It's probably in her interest if the place gets into trouble again with the CQC."

"Care Quality Commission? The regulators?"

"They were all over Broadmead last year. Pages of recommendations and warnings."

Jack thought about Shirley Woods. Maybe she was letting things slide to punch up her case against the Home, force a good settlement? Was she one of the bad guys in this after all?

"Thing is, Mr Brennan," said Leacock, "this is all very bad for business."

"Right. Guessing also that it's not so good for the residents, you never thought of that?"

"No, no, you're absolutely right; that's terrible of me to put it like that. But at heart, if the business is doing well, the staff are happy and so are the residents. It 'cascades' — that's the word."

"Okay. Now, why did you think I could help?"

"Obviously I need to know what's going on in that place. I don't want people suffering. I need somebody inside who can find the bad apples. Weed them out. Someone who can tell me what to do — because right now I'm at a loss."

Does this guy actually want sympathy? Jack thought.

He sat back in the deep sofa.

This wasn't what he'd expected. Was Leacock sincere? If so then the mess at Broadmead was just that. Not some kind of conspiracy, cover-up, exploitation.

Just a screw-up, understaffed, bad security, unlocked doors. Bad business, run by people who'd taken their eye of the ball.

And poor old Archy had died because nobody was really in charge.

Jack stood up.

"I'm not for hire, Mr. Leacock. And you don't need a

detective. What you need is a manager."

"But don't you see? The way this is structured, I can't just *hire* a manager, that has to be done by the Broadmead board—"

Jack didn't want to hear more about the complicated *architecture* of Richard Leacock's world that somehow prevented him from accepting or understanding responsibility.

"Thanks for the coffee, I'll make my own way out," said Jack. "No need for the butler."

Jack watched Leacock stand as if to shake hands, but Jack just turned and went out into the hallway. The butler was waiting anyway with his hat and coat and the front door already open.

Jack left without a word, and stepped out into the snow-covered drive towards his car.

He took a deep breath and looked around.

The sun had come out and the perfect white vista of English countryside looked pure and clean.

Felt good after all that garbage inside.

His whole life as a cop hinged on the good moments when he could in some small way right a wrong, find a killer, bring a felon to justice.

But cases like this — where people died because of sloppy thinking, laziness, weakness, moral cowardice?

Cases like this angered him, making him want to bring down whatever system — and whatever people — were responsible.

His phone rang — he saw it was Sarah. He put it to his ear.

"Hi Sarah."

"Hi Jack. Can you talk?"

"Sure."

"Couple of things."

"Go ahead."

"Alan rang, says the post mortem on Archy came up as expected. Hypothermia and heart failure."

"Figures."

"And Ellie rang me from the Ploughman's. Said they found an old bag of clothes where Reg was hiding in their car park. She thinks maybe it was his. Can you drop by if you're passing and pick it up? Could be something."

Strange, Jack thought. *What can an old bag of clothes have to do with any of this?*

Still, worth a look.

"Sure, will do."

"You okay, Jack?"

"Yeah, I'm good. Didn't come up with anything here. Unless you can factor in nobody really running the place."

"Oh. So, where are we?"

"We're at a dead end, Sarah. For now. No crime. Nothing to investigate. Nada."

"Really?" said Sarah. "I still think there's something wrong up at the home, Jack."

"Maybe. Maybe not. Maybe it's time for us to move on. Hey, there's still snow, take the kids tobogganing again, have some fun. Let the Quality... what is it called?"

"Quality Care Commission."

"Right. Maybe they know how to do *their* job."

"So, let it go, hmm?"

"Think so."

"Sure. Maybe see you at the weekend if it clears?"

"Be great. Come on over to the Goose, have some supper."

"Right. Bye Jack."

"See you …"

Jack put his phone away and climbed into the little Sprite. His breath misted the windshield and he wiped it with his gloved hand.

Come on spring, he thought as he started the engine and drove away down the elegant drive.

13.

A CHAT IN THE CHURCH

SARAH TRIED TO focus on work. If Jack thought that there was nothing they could do, no crime committed, he was probably right.

And yet — as she stared at the big screen in front of her, the layout for the Cherringham Children's Summer Play Scheme in progress — she couldn't shake the feeling that there *was* something wrong with all of it.

Archy dying in the blizzard, Reg wandering about, Nurse Woods about as defensive as they come.

Could Jack be wrong?

Whatever — now distracted, she certainly wasn't doing her best work.

The office phone rang, and Grace picked it up with a cheery "hello".

Sarah kept moving images around: a child smiling in swimming trunks, swings in motion, toddlers on a field attempting to kick a football.

"Right," Grace said. "Yes, she's here. And who shall I—?"

Sarah turned. Call obviously for her, someone who did not have her mobile.

"Okay, I can check. Please hold a moment."

Grace hit a button on the desk phone.

"Sarah, someone for you. A woman, bit of an accent. Says she needs to speak to you?"

"Who is it?"

"That's the thing. She won't say. Just wants to talk."

"Hope they don't want me to refinance my home, or buy a time share. I'll take it here."

Sarah hit the blinking button on her own desk phone.

SHE RECOGNISED THE voice immediately.

Ania.

And even on the phone, Sarah could feel the nurse's fear, the voice halting, a near-whisper.

"Sarah — I have things to tell you."

Just when she and Jack thought it was all over.

"Yes, Ania — what is it?"

"No. I can't, not now, not over the phone."

"Okay."

She saw Grace looking over, a quizzical look on her face.

"Um. How about we meet at the Ploughman's, or Huffington's—"

The "no" came fast.

"It must be someplace we can be alone."

Sarah knew that with the snowdrifts outside, a walk in the park wouldn't be an option.

"You could come to my office, it's just—"

Another quick no.

"Anybody might *see*. You're right in the village square."

And at that moment, Sarah felt some of Ania's fear. For the woman to be that nervous, that scared... maybe there were things for Sarah to be scared of as well.

So she tried to think where they might meet, where they would in all likelihood not be seen.

She only came up with one candidate.

"Ania — how about in the church, a pew at the back? Should be empty this time of day."

The woman hesitated.

Then: "Yes. I can meet you there. When?"

Sarah looked at Grace. "You okay holding down things here?"

"Sure."

Back to Ania: "In ten minutes?"

The woman on the other end of the line took a deep breath.

"Yes. I will see you there."

"Bye," Sarah said.

She put the phone down and got up from her desk and the now jumbled images of kids in summer.

Summer, she thought. *Cannot come soon enough.*

'Everything okay?" Grace said.

Her assistant had been so great about not asking questions when she and Jack got 'into' things. Most people would be dying of curiosity, but Grace was just supportive, and waited.

And when it was all over, Sarah would tell her all about it.

"Be gone for a bit. Not too sure how—"

"No worries. You okay, Sarah?"

Interesting.

That thought hadn't occurred to her, about any possibility of danger.

'I think so. Got my phone. Just need to have a chat with someone."

Grace nodded. "Be careful."

"Always," Sarah said.

Though she knew that wasn't quite true.

Grabbing her parka and wool hat, she hurried out of the office to the still-snowy streets outside.

ANIA WAS SITTING in the back row of pews, to the right, almost hidden by the font.

A few candles flickered in the racks at the front of the church; sunlight came through the stained-glass windows over the altar. But the rows of pews were dark and shadowy.

And apart from Ania — sitting there, seeing Sarah rush in — the place was empty.

Sarah walked to the right, and Ania slid in to make room for her.

When they spoke, both their voices were low.

Because they were in a church... or more from the fear in Ania's voice?

"Sarah, thank you for coming. I had to tell you. I just couldn't—"

The nurse turned away, looked to the front of the church.

Could be... she was someone who believed in the power of church, of a god, of prayer and the holiness of a place such as this?

In which case, this might be even harder for her to do.

"Ania — there's something you couldn't tell us, back at the home?"

Ania nodded. "No, someone might hear. Even now, I'm not sure."

Sarah reached out and patted the woman's hand. Cold. Sarah gave it a small squeeze.

"I only want to help the people in the home, I'm sure you do too," Sarah said.

Another nod. Ania again glanced at the pulpit, then turned back to Sarah.

"Yes. I know that, I can *feel* that. So, I will trust you and tell you."

Another deep breath. And she began.

"IT'S CRAIG."

Bingo, thought Sarah

"He knew about me, about my... problem."

"What problem is that?"

"My status. I'm not here legally, no work permit. I mean, I'm a fully certified nurse, but—"

"You don't have a permit from the government?"

Ania nodded.

"And Broadmead hired you anyway?"

"You've seen that place? They need people and they could get me cheap. That Miss Woods — she knew I would take the job and keep quiet. And I love the work, I love the people."

And Craig? Sarah wondered.

"But not everyone you worked with."

"Him? *Craig.* I know he doesn't have healthcare certification. But what does Woods care? No one is in charge in that place."

She looked away again.

Even though they both whispered, it still felt loud in the stillness of the quiet church, where there was not a sound.

"But he found out about me. That I have no permit."

A singe tear in Ania's right eye. She dabbed at it with the back of her hand.

This was hard for her.

Ania turned back to Sarah.

"He told me that if I didn't just let him do things, that he would tell the authorities about me. That I'd lose my job, be kicked out of the country."

Another dab.

"It's okay," Sarah said, feeling the words to be empty when things were quite clearly *not* okay. "What did he want Ania?"

"When we did the rounds and gave the residents their drugs, he would take some. Sometimes the resident didn't get all they were supposed to; other times he just made sure that we had more on the trolley than we needed."

"He needed you to look the other way?"

A nod. "'Just be quiet,'" he told me. "Be quiet, and he would stay quiet as well."

"You let him steal drugs?" Sarah said.

"Yes. He made me, threatened me. You understand, don't you?"

"Drugs like?"

"Benzodiazepine... 'benzos', he called them. Said he could always sell them. And the pain-killers, the Percocet, hydrocodone."

Now both eyes welled with tears, Ania's shame and fear immense in the quiet of the dark church.

Sarah put an arm on the woman's shoulder, and that was all Ania needed to begin crying full out, shaking as Sarah held her close.

UNTIL: "ANIA, THAT was blackmail. It was Craig who stole the drugs, not you."

But Sarah also knew that in any investigation, Ania would indeed lose more than her job.

And Sarah didn't want that to happen.

But now they had the evidence that something criminal was going on in that place. The big question, did it have something to do with Archy's death?

For now, Sarah didn't see a connection.

Ania's sobs had quietened a bit, though she still had to wipe away the tears.

"Look, Ania, I will need to share this with my friend."

A worried look crossed the nurse's face, a headshake.

Sarah squeezed Ania's hand. "You can trust him... like you've trusted me. We will need to do something about Craig, and we will do it in a way that doesn't hurt you."

Though Sarah wasn't exactly sure how that could be done.

But Ania nodded. "Yes. I will trust you."

And at that moment, Sarah heard steps behind them, someone clearing their throat.

How long had the person been there?

She turned to see Reverend Hewitt walk in. When he came abreast of the back pew, he turned and nodded to the two of them.

"Everything all right, Sarah... Ania?"

So he knew the nurse as well.

Sarah forced a smile. "Yes, Reverend. Just talking."

The vicar nodded, obviously guessing that the two women huddled at the back weren't "just talking".

"If there's anything I can do, do let me know."

Sarah nodded. Probably someone else they could both trust. But for now:

"Thank you, Reverend."

And he continued walking to the front of the church.

"I must get back," Ania said.

"You okay?" Sarah said.

Ania nodded. "I feel better, having told you."

Sarah gave her shoulders another squeeze. She just hoped that the nurse's trust wasn't misplaced.

"I should get back as well, but first…"

She took out a pen and a scrap of paper from her purse and wrote down her mobile number.

'If you need to talk again, my phone."

And Ania smiled. "Thank you."

And then — leaving Reverend Hewitt up front, now kneeling in prayer — they walked out of the dark church to the bright snow-covered grounds outside.

14.

A NIGHT AT HOME

"OKAY, JACK — can you see this?"

Sarah had no trouble finding Craig on Facebook. He hadn't bothered to make his photos and posts for "friends only" so she didn't have to do anything special.

With Daniel and Chloe both busy with school projects and homework — all delayed due to fun in the snow — she had called Jack.

After she'd updated him about her meeting with Ania, she suggested that they both look online, into the life of their new "friend", Craig.

"Brand new Subaru Forester. Nice wheels for a Care Assistant."

"Right, Jack, and look at the pictures. Those places, high-end restaurants in London, a few shots from that club Vertigo."

"Never been myself."

She laughed at that.

The thought of Jack in a London club?

Talk about a fish out of water.

"Okay," she said. "Craig obviously has cash. He supposedly lives out off the main road in a caravan park. But

I don't know — looks like he has an apartment in the city."

"Big HDTV. Nice. I think those windows overlook the river. Not too shabby."

"And his Facebook friends? Tough looking crowd. Some of them asking when he's 'next in town', looking forward to 'getting connected'. There's another: 'can't wait for my main man'. What does that all sound like to you?"

"That Craig is one popular guy — and I'm guessing that his popularity is due to the drugs he ferries from Broadmead to London."

"Jack. I had another thought."

"Go on."

"It's bad enough if he skims drugs out of the Home's supply. But if he's taking from the patients then that's dangerous. They actually need those drugs. I mean, he could have hurt some of those old people."

"Or will sooner or later."

"What do we do?"

"Think... well, thinking two things. Right now, all we really have is what Ania told you."

"I know."

"And we'd both like to protect her. She's just another victim. So we need more. And I think there's only one way to get it."

"Which is?"

"I need to break in. Really give the place a look over. See where he might hide the drugs, get a look at how they monitor who takes what, get into Woods' office. Real evidence, so we can nail Craig, and not Ania."

"And this isn't about Archy anymore?"

She waited for Jack to reply. Whenever he didn't answer right away, she knew he was looking at all the facts, all the theories before he answered.

It was a moment she had grown to look forward to.

"Don't be so sure. Archy and Reg's escape could still have been an accident — but we have that CCTV recording, Craig and someone. Then, Reg, out there in the snow with Archy. How does that all fit together?"

"And the answer is inside Broadmead Grange?"

"Yup. I'm going to sneak in tonight, and—"

"No."

"What do you mean?"

Sarah had to figure that Jack had also grown to understand how she "worked", how she thought.

So — no surprise ahead.

"*We're* going to break in. Together."

"I don't know, Sarah. Breaking-in is illegal, might be best—"

"Jack — better to have another pair of eyes, if only to keep watch in case someone comes by. The two of us in there, we can make quick work of it."

Then she had the thought it wasn't just the legality of it that concerned Jack.

If Craig was dealing, for big bucks, then who knows what he'd do to stay safe?

"Jack, we can be careful. But we're in this together, right?"

The two amigos.

Another pause.

"Okay, you got it, Miss Marple. Break-in at Broadmead it is, for the two of us. Dress warm, dress in black. The Sprite is good to go, so I'll swing by and pick you up."

"Great."

Sarah could feel her heart thumping.

"I'll make sure the kids are settled, noses in books; they've got school tomorrow."

Jack laughed. "Bet they're thrilled. See you in ten."

"See you soon."

Sarah ended the call and checked her battery. Seventy per cent. Should be enough. And she went to her bedroom to look for the darkest and warmest clothes she could find.

DRIVING OUT TO Broadmead, Sarah saw a big black plastic bag in the back behind the seats. A strong smell came from the bag.

"Laundry?"

"What? Oh, that. The clothes they found, near the Ploughman's."

"That smell — it's aftershave."

"Yeah, strong."

"No. I mean, I know that smell. In Broadmead yesterday, I smelled it on Reg. When I talked to him in the chapel."

He turned to her. "Interesting."

Sarah reached back and pulled out a pair of thermal leggings from the bag.

"Thermal leggings. I don't understand it."

"If they're Reg's, then I don't either."

"Want a deeper sniff?"

Jack laughed. "No, I believe you."

She pulled another article from the plastic bag. A matching thermal shirt.

"Expensive stuff."

"Well, if it *is* Reg's... strange." Jack slowed the car. "Okay, going to park ahead."

Jack pulled the Sprite over to the side where cars could be off the road, nearly hidden in the deep banks of ploughed snow.

Lights off, they got out of the sports car.

IT HAD STARTED to snow again, and a stiff breeze sent swirls of the now crystalline stuff dancing around Jack.

With the car hidden, he led the way on a snowy path, crouch-walking closer to Broadmead.

Jack had done this kind of thing many times before.

Sneaking up to a Red Hook warehouse filled with drugs and guns, guarded by an army of thugs trained in Colombia.

Or zeroing in on a mob boss's quiet street in Queens, a summer night, but with the Don's bodyguards on the lookout... as a specially trained team under Jack circled the place.

So, while this was certainly different, it wasn't new.

But for Sarah?

And yet, when he looked back, her eyes catching her scant light, black ski trousers, dark blue skull cap, she looked like she could be an undercover cop pulling off a raid in NYC.

Maybe she missed her calling! he thought.

She came closer to Jack; both of them crouched low behind a scraggly bush that — if in the light — wouldn't give them much cover.

But the outside lighting of the Home hadn't been upgraded, and the few giant floods only cast pale milky pools just around the periphery of the gothic building.

"What do you think?" Sarah whispered.

Jack looked at the building.

They squatted to the right of the entrance, with a clear view of the car park. Most of it had been ploughed, and with four or five cars parked there, Jack guessed that tonight more workers would be on duty.

"Won't be so quiet in there this time. Was hoping the place would still be on skeleton staff."

"How about that back entrance? The one you saw on the CCTV?"

"Right. Good idea. Opening and shutting that door didn't trigger any alarms. Course, we'll be caught on the camera. But if we find what I think we will find, none of that will matter."

"We'll find it," Sarah said.

Amazing confidence, he thought.

He wasn't so sure. Someone like Craig could be good at covering his tracks.

And just as he thought that, the front door of Broadmead Grange opened and Craig himself emerged. Jack watched as the young care worker, dressed just in a T-shirt and jeans, pinged a key fob, hurried over to a big black SUV and opened the trunk.

"Waddya know," said Jack quietly. "Mr. Subaru himself."

"Looks like he's thirsty," whispered Sarah.

Jack peered through the gently falling snow. Craig had retrieved a bottle of what looked like Scotch from the car. He slammed the trunk shut and headed back inside.

Jack waited till Craig had gone in and the drive was quiet again.

"Ready?" he said, turning to her. "Jack — what do we do if someone spots us?"

He nodded. "Hope it's Ania? And if it's someone else, well, I imagine sometimes people come here to see their relatives even after closing hours."

"Got it. Act natural. Just here visiting."

He grinned at that. *If only it was that easy.*

"Set?"

"Yup. My knees are going to feel this in the morning."

"Tell me about it."

And Jack, staying low, away from the light, headed right, then circled to the back, where he hoped that they could get inside Broadmead Grange... and it would reveal all its secrets.

15.

A SURPRISING DISCOVERY

SARAH WATCHED JACK fish out a thin piece of metal from a pocket of his bulky coat.

She kept her head down. While she knew that they were now on camera, that was no reason to make it easy to ID them. If anyone was watching the footage, they'd see this break-in but wouldn't be able to see their faces.

But Jack said that based on seeing the "security" operation and how cavalier Nurse Woods was about it, the video probably usually went unwatched.

If not, they could expect to hear a siren screaming this way in minutes.

Jack began working the piece of metal into the jam where the door met the frame.

"Hmm," he said.

"Not working?"

"Has a metal plate over the outside, makes getting to the bolt mechanism tricky."

"Impossible?"

He looked back at her. "No. *Tricky*. Not impossible. There is a very subtle difference, Sarah."

So cold standing there. Despite layers of clothes and the

hat, the steady wind seemed to find its way to bare skin.

Maybe — she thought — they'd be stuck here, adventure over.

Though, knowing Jack…

"Okay — let me try something different."

She watched him go above the lock mechanism with the thin metal piece, then down, slipping past the faceplate protecting the bolt.

"Okay, good."

Jack's gloved hand wobbled back and forth, until she heard metal scratching on metal. It was like he was fishing — and just now had caught something.

A different *clicking* noise, and suddenly, as if someone was inviting them in, the door popped open a fraction of an inch.

For a moment, Sarah thought that — God! — someone had come back here, for a smoke, or to leave, and stumbled upon them.

But Jack pulled the unlocked door open another inch or so. Looked in.

"All clear. Stay close. Just in case."

She had no intention of doing otherwise.

And then Jack fully opened the door, and they walked inside Broadmead, their entire break-in caught on camera.

SARAH STUCK CLOSE to Jack as they entered a dark hall. Where were they in the building?

She didn't have a clue.

There seemed to be rooms ahead, doors closed. Empty maybe — or housing sleeping residents.

"Pretty spooky," she whispered.

Jack didn't answer, but he turned, nodded. A small smile.

Right, she thought. *Best we stay quiet.*

Until she saw a man come out of a room, backlit by the bedroom light, flannel robe, slippers, hair shooting off the top of his head as though he'd touched an electrical socket.

"Oh, are you here for the party?"

Jack stopped.

They could keep walking, Sarah guessed. But even someone with dementia could trigger an alarm.

"Why, yes," Jack said quietly.

"I do hope they have those nice cakes."

Jack nodded, another smile to Sarah.

"You know the ones?"

"Sure," Jack said.

"Chocolate sponge and white frosting. Yes!"

Then the old man turned and looked away, his face — confused now — catching some of the light spilling from his room.

"Or is it the other way around? White cake, and chocolate... chocolate…"

Jack gave the man a pat on the shoulder. "We'll make sure that we have both."

Big smile and the man turned back to his room, happy that he had imaginary cakes from an imaginary party to look forward to.

And when the hallway was empty, they continued on.

UNTIL THEY SAW Woods' office ahead, the hall lighting again low, probably to remind the residents to stay in their rooms.

Then a door opened — a supply room, and backing out … *Ania.*

She turned and saw Jack and Sarah. Jack quickly put his hand to his lips. Even at this distance, Ania looked worried. But she nodded, turned away and hurried down the corridor.

Leaving the way to Woods' office clear.

When they got to the office, Jack gave the doorknob a twist. Locked. But this door he had open in seconds.

And Sarah followed him into the room, pulling the door shut behind them. For now, they were out of sight, with time to see what could be hidden here, hidden... and found.

SARAH IMMEDIATELY WENT to the computer on Woods' desk, while she saw Jack go to a stack of filing cabinets and crouch down.

Each of us, she thought, *about to dig into things in the way we know best.*

The computer came to life, and Sarah started to see how she could enter the home's protected administrative site.

"One of these days," Jack said, "you'll have to explain to me exactly how you do that. It's a bit scary."

At the same moment, the lock on the bottom filing cabinet popped out and open.

"And you'll have to repay the favour by showing me how you do that."

"This? Piece of cake. All you need is a paper clip."

"Right. Anyone can do it, hmm?" Sarah said grinning.

Jack started rifling through the files.

Sarah hit some keys, bypassing whatever encryption the site used, and then: "I'm in."

And it was all there, the names and histories of the residents, employee records, billing accounts.

Nothing about drugs though.

Maybe that was in a paper file, and Jack would find it.

But she quickly brought up Archy's case history.

The records showed that the old man had years of hospital stays, other homes, and the progress of his Alzheimer's severe and inevitable, until he'd ended up here, confused and wandering out into a blizzard.

Then — something interesting.

Old Archy had done time in Belmarsh prison. Didn't say what he was in for — perhaps, those records were confidential, locked.

But it looked like Archy hadn't exactly been a choirboy.

"Jack — take a look."

Holding a handful of manila folders, Jack walked over. "Archy's an ex-con. Wow."

"Hard to believe," said Sarah.

"Even bad guys grow old, end up in homes," said Jack.

"Whatever he did, he paid for it in prison," said Sarah.

"Looks like a five-year stretch," said Jack. "You got to do more than have your fingers in the till for that."

Then: "Can you get Reg's record up?"

"Sure." She kept looking at Jack. "You think—?"

Jack smiled. "Not sure what I think Sarah. But let's see what Reg's story is while we're in."

Sarah turned back to the monitor, and searched for Reg's details.

"Here we go. And—"

"What?"

Jack leaned over her shoulder.

"Archy's records showed a long history of dealing with Alzheimer's. But Reg? Months ago he went into Royal Derby Hospital for gall bladder surgery. No mention of anything else before that. But then notes here about sudden erratic behaviour, see... 'signs of rapid onset dementia'."

"Rapid?"

"Yes, and look: 'patient's solicitor requested that only Broadmead be considered for convalescent care'."

"Only Broadmead? I have to think there are better places than this house of horrors."

Sarah scrolled through the rest of the information on patient Reg's file. The she stopped.

"Oh God, Jack. This is too weird."

"What am I looking at?"

She pointed at a line. "Reg's previous medical history had been transferred from Belmarsh prison to Derby, the same—"

"—prison that housed Archy. Though, it looks like Reg had a much longer stay."

"Decades. Looks like Reg and Archy must have been old pals."

"Or at least in the same line of business, huh?" said Jack.

She stopped then. "I don't see what this has to do with Craig, or drugs. But this—" she turned to Jack, "is something, yes?"

A nod. "Could be. For now, let's stay on track with how they handle their drug records here. I'm thinking that for anything dodgy, they wouldn't want a digital record, not when there are hackers like you out there."

Sarah rolled her eyes. "*Hacker?* Hardly. I could make all these systems so much more secure!"

She watched Jack put a pile of folders down on the other side of the desk, and begin going through them.

Could someone come in here? she thought.

Could they even be sure that Woods was gone for the night?

She just hoped that whatever they were looking for they'd find it soon.

JACK WORKED FAST — this was a task he'd done many times before. He knew what he was looking for: the drug dispensing files, but also the drug purchasing folder too.

Each file he skimmed through, he stacked on one side.

But the paper files were dense. Invoices, training, security, staff correspondence — there was stuff in here from years back before Heathstone had bought Broadmead.

He looked past Sarah at the CCTV monitor which showed the exterior of the home. Nothing moving outside. Shame there weren't cameras in the corridors. Any second now that door could open and …

"This is going to take some time," he said.

"How long we got?"

"Another five minutes and I'll start feeling edgy," said Jack. "Why don't you copy everything you can — just in case."

"I'm on it already," said Sarah, slotting a flash drive into the computer.

Jack picked up the pile of folders, dropped them back in the filing cabinet and shut the drawer. Then he slid open the next drawer above, took out another stack of files and joined Sarah at the desk.

Purchasing orders — he was in the right place. And then he hit the folder he needed.

"This'll do nicely," he said, quickly scanning the contents. "Monthly totals of all pharmaceuticals purchased, going back a couple of years. Now we just need to find out how they dispensed them."

He took the folder back to the filing cabinet and got the

next batch out of the drawer.

As he returned to the desk, a movement on the CCTV screen caught his eye. He peered at the top quarter of the TV: through the softly falling snow a figure was walking towards the front door of Broadmead Grange. As they approached the camera, Jack recognised the face.

"Sarah," he said, nodding to the screen. "We've got houseguests."

Sarah turned — and Jack could see the alarm in her face.

"Shirley Woods," she said.

"Did I say five minutes?" he said. "Make that three."

His hands flew through the files, and then—

"Got it."

"Dispensing sheets?"

"Yep, all signed by Ania," he said. "Patient by patient, going back to last year."

"So we can see if dosages have changed?"

"Exactly," said Jack, rolling the papers and slotting them deep in his winter jacket. "The proof we're looking for — I hope."

He heard a door slam deep within the building.

"Time we got out of here," he said. "You got the download?"

He watched Sarah ease the digital stick out, then run through the shutdown.

"I have now."

"Let's go," he said.

"Back to the car?" said Sarah.

"Not quite yet," said Jack. "I think we ought to put the squeeze on our friend Craig before we go."

"Looking forward to that already," said Sarah.

What a partner, thought Jack. *Like I never retired.*

He flicked the desk light off, tidied the drawers of the filing cabinet and gently opened the door, aware of Sarah close behind him.

He looked each way down the dimly lit corridor — empty. He checked Sarah was ready and slipped out of the office. As soon as Sarah was out too, he shut the door gently behind him. It locked automatically with a click as he closed it.

And then he heard another door opening, just yards away. He could see Shirley Woods emerging, her back luckily towards them.

He grabbed Sarah and pulled her quickly across the corridor into the dark shadows of a stairwell. He held his breath — if Woods turned to go up these stairs then the game was up.

As he watched, the sister strode by, head up, busy, busy. She paused at her office, took out a key, unlocked the door and went in — all without seeing them.

"Guess it's our lucky day," said Jack. He could hear Sarah's steady breathing in and out.

Tense moment. Then:

"What are we waiting for?" she whispered with a smile.

So, with Sarah at his side, he headed down the corridor deeper into the Home to find Craig.

16.

A LOVELY CUPPA

SARAH FOLLOWED JACK down the corridor. Although she felt lost, it seemed that Jack knew where he was going.

The place was eerily quiet. But as they turned a corner, she could hear the sound of hushed male voices and the clink of glass on bottle. She smelled cigarette smoke too.

At the end of this corridor she could see a half-open door, and light spilled out.

Just ahead of her, Jack paused and turned: "Kitchens," he said. "And if I'm not mistaken, that sounds like our old friend Craig."

She followed him to the door, and pressed against the wall right next to him so she could listen to the low, muttered conversation in the kitchen.

"Top-up?"

"Large one, this time Craig — none of your bleedin' country measures."

The other voice was older, gravelly. Sarah thought she recognised it, but couldn't quite place it. She heard the glasses clinking again. Then the older voice continued. Craig was clearly getting some careers advice.

"Like I was saying — you got a choice, son. Big frog, little pond — or little frog, big pond. What you got to remember is — cheers — little frogs get bigger don't they?"

"Easy for you to say. You got connections," said Craig.

"I'll make 'em your connections, too."

"I dunno. I've got a nice deal here. Why muck it up?"

"Can't go on forever. Gotta move on. Move *up*. Big city — big margins."

"Big risks though."

"Risks is life, son. Don't get nowhere without it."

"You think I can cut it?"

"Sure. You'll be working for me. Not just skimmin' benzos off a trolley. I mean the real deal. Import. Export. Your own little patch."

"Gotta admit, this place stinks. And all these effin' zombies — I hate them, sometimes, I just want to punch 'em, know what I mean?"

Sarah never saw Jack move faster — she watched as he pushed the door open as if it wasn't there and strode ahead of her into the kitchen.

She followed him into the kitchen as everything seemed to happen at once. The door banged back hard on its hinges and she saw a table at the far end of the room with Craig now looking up surprised, then pushing his chair backwards and getting up fast, retreating and hurling a glass at Jack as he approached …

Jack sounding so angry.

This was new.

"Craig — what did I tell you about using that word?"

"Whoa, you! How did you—"

And Sarah now seeing in Jack's hand his old NYPD nightstick suddenly appearing—

Where the hell was he keeping that hidden? she thought.

And as Craig backed away against the big cooking ranges, cowering, she saw almost in slow motion who was sitting at the table quietly observing this mayhem: Reg Povey.

Reg. Glass of scotch in one hand, cigarette in the other, feet up on the table. Dressed not in pyjamas or nightgown, but in micro-fleece and jeans.

Reg. Not baffled dementia patient, surely…

But lean, mean-looking, wily old man.

Hardened criminal — according to those records.

Meanwhile Jack had hold of Craig by the T-shirt and was dragging him across to a chair by the back door.

"I'm sorry, I'm sorry, I'm sorry — I didn't do nothin'," Craig was saying over and over again, his hands on his head.

Like he's a prisoner in a war film, thought Sarah.

"Shut up, sit down and don't move," said Jack to Craig.

Sarah realised that everything had gone quiet. The rush of action finished as quickly as it had started. She was breathing heavily.

"Dear, oh dear," said Reg, flicking ash into a saucer. "Cops. Same the whole world over. Can't just walk into a room politely, eh?"

"You haven't got dementia," said Sarah, thinking aloud.

"Oh, I have, darling," said Reg. "Been diagnosed. By a proper doctor."

"That must have cost you," said Jack. Sarah could see him keeping one eye on Craig in his chair and now sizing up Reg.

"Now that's a slur, Jack. Doctors don't lie," said Reg. "Just like cops. Isn't that right?"

"Why pretend to have dementia?" said Sarah. "I don't understand …"

Sarah watched Reg lean across to the bottle of Scotch on the table and pour himself another shot.

"Sarah, you got a signal in here?" said Jack.

She pulled out her phone, checked — and shook her head.

"Bad luck, sweetheart," said Reg. "Coverage here is crap. It's played havoc with my bookie."

Sarah looked at Jack and shrugged. She knew that what he'd really meant was — time to call the cops.

Going to have to play for time, she thought.

"Why did you come here Reg?" she said quickly.

But it was Jack who answered.

"It was for Archy, wasn't it, Reg?"

Sarah felt confused.

What was Jack saying?

"But I've seen his records," she said to Reg. "He was very ill. You couldn't help him."

Jack took a step closer to Reg, nightstick still in his hand. And Reg nodded.

"I didn't want to *help* him, love," said Reg, smiling.

That smile... scary, she thought.

"I wanted to kill the bastard."

"He put you inside, didn't he?" said Jack. "Long stretch, huh?"

"Could say that. Twenty years," said Reg.

"For something you didn't do?" said Sarah.

Her blood chilled as Reg laughed again.

"Do me a favour — of course I *did* it. But he was supposed to go down for it, not me."

"He did a deal with the cops?" said Jack.

"Exactly," said Reg. "And I've had to wait a very long time to get my own back."

"But you managed it," said Jack.

"With pleasure," said Reg.

"Got yourself in here, fooled everyone, then just led him

out into the snow to die."

"Piece of cake," said Reg. "Wasn't the original plan, of course. I wanted it to hurt a bit more. But I thought — all that snow — nobody would ever know."

"The perfect murder," said Sarah.

"It would have been," said Jack. "If it hadn't been for Craig's little drugs scam."

"Ah," said Reg, stubbing out his cigarette. "So, that's what brought you back. I thought I'd got rid of you."

She watched as Reg pushed back his chair and stood up. He smiled at her again — and the smile made her feel queasy.

"I should thank you really, for giving me a lift back from the pub the other day," he said. "Very decent of you."

Sarah wondered what was going to happen.

Jack stood looking immoveable by the back door, his nightstick steady. Craig sat with his hands between his knees looking scared.

"Course, I'm not quite as feeble as I look," said Reg. "Not much to do in prison. Gotta work out, stay fit, isn't that right, Jack?"

"You can't get away," said Jack.

But Reg didn't seem to be listening. He turned to Craig: "So what's it going to be, Craig me old son? Big city or small time?"

"God. I don't know, Reg," said Craig, looking nervously at Jack.

"Don't worry about him," said Reg. "Ex-cop. Yank. Loser."

Sarah looked at Jack. What was happening? Then—

"What in heaven's name is going on in here?"

Sarah turned — it seemed everyone turned — to see Shirley Woods striding across the kitchen towards them.

112

"Smoking! Drinking! Craig — I want you in my office right now! And Reg, time you were back in your bed, my dear. Meanwhile, you two had better explain just—"

Sarah saw Shirley suddenly stop in her tracks, her mouth open wide — and for the second time that night everything happened fast.

She looked to her side — and Reg had pulled a butcher's knife from a block by the cooker and was backing over to join Craig.

"Reg?" said Shirley. "That's a very sharp knife, my dear…"

She took a few steps away, instinctively. She saw Jack do the same.

"Whoa, Reg," said Jack. "Sure you want to do that?"

"Get the damn car warmed up," said Reg to Craig.

Sarah could see that Craig was just as stunned as she was.

"Bright lights, big city, Craig," said Reg, lifting Craig to his feet. "Move it. Back the car up here to the door."

Reg slipped the catch of the back door and pushed the young carer out into the darkness.

"Reg Povey, put that knife down right now!" said Shirley Woods.

"Sorry, Sister, no can do," said Reg, moving the knife in an arc which seemed to threaten all of them. "Now put your phones on the table, please."

"Jack?" said Sarah.

She saw Jack shake his head to her and then reach into his pocket and put his phone on the table. She followed suit. Next to her, Shirley Woods did the same.

Through the kitchen windows Sarah saw the lights of Craig's car as it backed up through the thick snow into the courtyard.

"It's been special," said Reg, slipping the phones into his pocket. "One thing though, Sister — the food here's worse than prison and that takes some doing, I can tell ya."

Sarah watched as he backed out through the door. She heard the car door slam, then the Subaru slid away through the snow and was gone.

She turned to Jack:

"What are we waiting for?" she said. "Let's go after them!"

"All in good time," said Jack, folding his nightstick away calmly. "Sister Woods — can we borrow your car?"

"On one condition," she said. "You come straight back here and you tell me just what the hell is going on and what happened to my patient."

"Deal," said Jack politely.

"It's the Corolla out front," she said, handing Jack the keys. "Don't wreck it, and put some petrol in it too while you're at it."

"Why, thank you ma'am," said Jack, heading for the door. "Sarah?"

And Sarah followed him out into the courtyard.

This had to be the slowest car chase she'd ever been in.

Come to think of it, she thought, *it's also the first.*

JACK STEERED THE Corolla carefully down the High Street.

It had stopped snowing but there was still a good foot of snow lying on the road. The village was quiet — people staying at home, he guessed, waiting for the big thaw which was due tomorrow.

"Takes me back, driving this," he said to Sarah. "Katherine used to have one back in New York."

"Oh really?" said Sarah. "I guess in the Sprite we could go a bit faster, maybe catch them up?"

Jack smiled to himself.

"Oh, we don't need to catch them up," he said.

He looked out of the side window at the Ploughman's as they went past. The lights were on. Nothing kept the regulars away, not even a dark and snowy night.

"We don't?" said Sarah. "But if they get to London, the police will never find them." ·

Jack slowed as they crossed the old bridge. At this time of night the toll booth was closed but the road narrowed and he needed to be careful as they slipped through.

"'Fraid they're not going to get to London," said Jack, as they rounded the first of the two sharp curves in the road.

"You sure?"

"I am now," he said, reaching forward to put the hazard lights on and pulling in to the side of the road. "Look."

He pointed out of Sarah's side window and she wound down the window so they could see clearly.

"Yikes!" she said.

"Wow," he said. "Craig was going even faster than I expected."

In the beam from the headlights, he could see the Subaru's wheel tracks deep in the snow. The tracks crossed the ditch at the side of the road, went straight through a hole in the thick hedge and right the way up to the edge of the little stream that crossed the meadow.

They ended in the black shape of the Subaru, upside down in the snow, lights still on, the roof crushed.

"You think they're okay?" said Sarah, rushing to open the door.

"Unfortunately, yes," said Jack, climbing out to join her.

"Air bags will have done their job."

"Now I see why you took your time," said Sarah.

"Knowing Craig and knowing this corner?" said Jack, "It was a no-brainer."

"We going down to get them out?"

"You kidding?" said Jack. "After what he called me? Loser? Yank? No, we'll flag down a car, phone for help. Let 'em stew."

"You must have been called worse than that, Jack."

"Plenty of times," he said. "But you know what really hurt? Ex-cop. That — was below the belt."

And he stepped into the road to flag down an approaching car from the village.

17.

IT'S THE THOUGHT THAT COUNTS

Sarah watched Odelia blow out the candles on her birthday cake, then all the residents cheered.

She looked around at the happy faces — so different from when she and Jack had last been in the home.

The residents were gathered round the big dining table with party hats on, there was music playing and the food smelled delicious.

At least a dozen nurses and carers were involved and joining in the party. She could see Ania, face happy, joining in a group singing in the corner.

"Ninety-three today!" said Beth, giving her grandmother a kiss.

"Just seven more till your telegram from the Queen," said Sarah.

She watched Jack raise his cup of tea: "Here's to you Odelia, and thanks for your help when we needed it."

"You want any more help with crime-busting, just give me a call, Jack," said Odelia.

"Oh yeah?" said Jack. "As it happens, we might have an undercover job coming up, I'll keep you in the loop."

"You've been watching too much *24*, Gran," said Beth.

"Heck, we couldn't have cracked it without her," said Jack.

"And I am glad that you did," said Shirley Woods, joining them at the table. "It certainly put a rocket up the management here."

"Funny what a little bad publicity can do to a good investment," said Sarah.

Shirley moved in confidentially to Sarah: "I still feel guilty that I didn't know how bad things were. It was on my watch."

Sarah saw Jack lean over: "You were in an impossible position Shirley and it wasn't your fault."

"I should have seen what Craig was doing with the drugs — and the nurses."

"Forget Craig," said Jack. "As well as the drugs charges, he's on conspiracy to murder. He won't be back."

"So he helped kill Archy?" said Shirley.

"He bought the thermals so Reg could lead Archy into the woods," said Jack.

"You think we should have been more suspicious at the beginning, Jack?" said Sarah.

She watched him consider this.

"I guess we all might have been. If we did make a mistake it was to assume that just because Reg was old and frail he was an innocent victim."

"It gives me the chills to think he'd murdered before," said Shirley.

"Don't forget — so had Archy," said Jack. "Alan Rivers told me he had three, maybe four alleged murders back on his file."

Sarah looked around the room at the other twenty or so residents.

"It's easy to forget that they're all just... people. No different from people everywhere. Just older."

"Too right," said Shirley. "And now that nice Mr. Leacock has doubled the staff budget, I do believe we can treat them like that."

Sarah lifted her cup of tea in a mock toast: "To Hearthstone Investments, Jack?"

He shook his head, raising his cup too. "No. To Ania and the staff — and a new start."

And as Sarah raised her cup of tea, she thought how much her time with Jack had been a new start for her too.

NEXT IN THE SERIES:

CHERRINGHAM

A COSY CRIME SERIES

PLAYING DEAD

Matthew Costello & Neil Richards

When Cherringham Drama Society invite a local TV celebrity to direct their Christmas show, they get more publicity than they bargained for.

Someone's out to sabotage the event, and rehearsals spin into chaos.

Jack and Sarah are asked to investigate and soon discover that there's a darker mystery taking place behind the scenes...

ABOUT THE AUTHORS

Matthew Costello (US-based) and **Neil Richards** (UK) have been writing TV scripts together for more than twenty years. The best-selling Cherringham series is their first collaboration as fiction writers: since its first publication as ebooks and audiobooks the series has sold over a million copies.

Matthew is the author of many successful novels, including *Vacation* (2011), *Home* (2014) and *Beneath Still Waters* (1989), which was adapted by Lionsgate as a major motion picture. He has written for The Disney Channel, BBC, SyFy and has also written dozens of bestselling games including the critically acclaimed *The 7th Guest*, *Doom 3*, *Rage* and *Pirates of the Caribbean*.

Neil has worked as a producer and writer in TV and film, creating scripts for BBC, Disney, and Channel 4, and earning numerous Bafta nominations along the way. He's also written script and story for over 20 video games including *The Da Vinci Code* and *Broken Sword*.